The Girl I Saved on the Train Turned Out to Be My Childhood Friend

Kennoji

Illustration by Fly

The Girl I Saved on the Train Turned Out to Be My Childhood Friend

3

Kennoji

Illustration by Fly

YEN
ON
New York

The Girl I Saved on the Train Turned Out to Be My Childhood Friend ③

Kennoji

Translation by Sergio Avila
Cover art by Fly

This book is a work of fiction. Names, characters, places, and incidents are the product of the author's imagination or are used fictitiously. Any resemblance to actual events, locales, or persons, living or dead, is coincidental.

CHIKAN SARESOU NI NATTEIRU S-KYU BISHOUJO WO TASUKETARA TONARI NO SEKI NO OSANANAJIMI DATTA volume 3
Copyright © 2020 Kennoji
Illustrations copyright © 2020 Fly
All rights reserved.
Original Japanese edition published in 2020 by SB Creative Corp.
This English edition is published by arrangement with SB Creative Corp., Tokyo in care of Tuttle-Mori Agency, Inc., Tokyo.

English translation © 2022 by Yen Press, LLC

Yen Press, LLC supports the right to free expression and the value of copyright. The purpose of copyright is to encourage writers and artists to produce the creative works that enrich our culture.

The scanning, uploading, and distribution of this book without permission is a theft of the author's intellectual property. If you would like permission to use material from the book (other than for review purposes), please contact the publisher. Thank you for your support of the author's rights.

Yen On
150 West 30th Street, 19th Floor
New York, NY 10001

Visit us at yenpress.com ✧ facebook.com/yenpress ✧ twitter.com/yenpress ✧ yenpress.tumblr.com ✧ instagram.com/yenpress

First Yen On Edition: October 2022
Edited by Yen On Editorial: Shella Wu, Anna Powers
Designed by Yen Press Design: Wendy Chan

Yen On is an imprint of Yen Press, LLC.
The Yen On name and logo are trademarks of Yen Press, LLC.

The publisher is not responsible for websites (or their content) that are not owned by the publisher.

Library of Congress Cataloging-in-Publication Data
Names: Kennoji, author. | Fly, 1963- illustrator. | Avila, Sergio, translator.
Title: The girl I saved on the train turned out to be my childhood friend / Kennoji ; illustration by Fly ; translation by Sergio Avila.
Other titles: Chikan saresou ni natteiru s-kyu bishoujo wo tasuketara tonari no seki no osananajimi datta. English
Description: First Yen On edition. | New York, NY : Yen On, 2021–
Identifiers: LCCN 2021039082 | ISBN 9781975336998 (v. 1 ; pbk.) | ISBN 9781975337018 (v. 2 ; pbk.) | ISBN 9781975337032 (v. 3 ; pbk.)
Subjects: CYAC: Love—Fiction. | LCGFT: Light novels.
Classification: LCC PZ7.1.K507 Gi 2021 | DDC [Fic]—dc23
LC record available at https://lccn.loc.gov/2021039082

ISBNs: 978-1-9753-3703-2 (paperback)
        978-1-9753-3704-9 (ebook)

1 2022

LSC-C

Printed in the United States of America

It was a morning like any other. I was on my way to school, on the train with my childhood friend Hina Fushimi.

"C'mon, don't look so down."

"I can't help it... Crowded trains suck."

I didn't like them, either, but Fushimi had her own reasons—she was nearly molested on one. Fortunately, nothing happened because I spotted the guy and called him out before he could do anything, although I didn't know it was her. After that, we started talking again for the first time since middle school, hanging out, and even going to and from school just like this. We were your typical pair of childhood friends.

"Hey, Ryou, how about we take the train thirty minutes earlier from now on?"

"No way. I won't be able to wake up for that."

"Aw..."

That was the second time she'd made that request. Last time, I told her she could do that on her own, and she got really upset. I'd just thought that was best for both of us. She wanted an empty train. I wanted to sleep longer. Why not?

Fushimi was in a bad mood for the rest of that day. She didn't tell me any of the answers to the questions the teachers asked me (as she usually does) or lend me lead for my mechanical pencil, and she refused to show me her notes.

...Listing all that just shows how hopeless I am, huh...?

Anyway, for whatever reason, my answer clearly wasn't the right one that day. That much I learned.

"It's too far away to bike, too…"

I don't like crowded trains, either. I'd at least like a strap to hang on to, though a seat would be better, of course. But if it's between this and having to wake up earlier, I'd take the crowds any day.

Fushimi, as close as possible to me without actually touching me, tilted her head. "You've tried it before?"

"Yeah, just one time. It took about forty minutes."

I could handle biking through the rain or the summer heat or the winter cold for twenty minutes, maybe, but not double that.

"On a bike, huh…," Fushimi whispered. "We could go side by side and chat on our way to school. Sounds nice."

For forty whole minutes?

The train then turned with a slight curve, adding pressure to my back. I straightened up to resist it. Couldn't let Fushimi be crushed.

She stared at me.

"…What?"

"Hee-hee. Nothing. Thanks." She grinned. I looked away.

I'd bumped into her many times due to the train's swaying, and every time, I wondered how it was possible for a girl's body to be so soft. And so fragrant.

The train stopped; people got off, and new passengers got on. We still had three stations left.

I tried to keep my mind calm, when I saw a girl wearing a school uniform I'd never seen before. She was standing just two meters away.

In crowded trains, most men tried to stay as far away as they could from women, to avoid being falsely accused as gropers, but there was this old guy standing unnaturally close behind her.

At that moment, I had no idea that girl was Fushimi's and my childhood friend, Ai Himejima.

©Fly

"Fushimi, hold on for a sec."

"Huh? Why...?"

I ignored Fushimi's question and made my way through the train. Everyone was glaring at me, but I ignored them.

I forced myself between the girl and the man, and just as I thought the day was saved once again, she grabbed me by the arm and pulled me off the train at the next station.

"...You again?" The railway officer looked at me suspiciously from the other side of the steel desk.

"It's not like I'm here because I want to be."

It was the same station where I'd pursued the guy who almost groped Fushimi.

A month and a half had gone by since then, and now I was once again being interrogated for poking my nose in yet another molestation case.

"So you've saved another high school girl from a groper, Takamori."

"Yup."

The one difference this time around was that the childhood friend in question and I had drifted apart because she transferred schools.

"...So where's that girl?"

"She...ran away."

Yup. As soon as Ai Himejima realized it was me, she booked it out of there.

"Again?"

"I mean..."

"I go all the way to the train platform hearing about some molester, and when I get there, I find you instead of a victim or an offender." He sighed, then stood up, turning away from me. "You sure it's not you? I won't tell anybody. Just be honest here."

You're not tricking me into getting arrested.

"Close your eyes, and if you did it, raise your hand."

What is this, a grade-school class meeting to figure out who broke a rule?

"I'm telling you, I stopped him. She just got it wrong."

My phone started vibrating. I took it out of my pocket and saw I had a text from Fushimi. I guessed she was worried about me, after being forced off the train.

Just like last time, I told the officer what the offender looked like and what he was doing.

"And um, sorry, but could you call the school to say I'll be late again, please?"

"Yeah, yeah," he said with another sigh.

I gave him the number, and he dialed it using the office's phone.

Since I was a recurring truant, if I called the school myself, they'd suspect I was lying.

Once finally released, I took the train again, totally empty compared to just before, and headed to school.

I had spoken to Ai two times since she transferred, through letters.

"I'll write you a letter, so please send me a reply, okay?" she had said back then, and then the letter arrived. I'd said yes, so I had to send one back.

Fushimi, Ai, Mana, and I hung out together all the time.

What is she doing here now, though? What if...she's back?

And it turned out I was right.

I arrived right before first period and saw that everyone in the classroom was restless. They didn't even notice or care that I was late.

"Why did you get off the train so suddenly?" Except for Fushimi.

"Hey, Fushimi, remember Ai?"

"Yeah. You mean Himejima, right?"

I nodded and told her about the girl who nearly got molested. "That was Ai."

"Huh?! Seriously? Then maybe it is her!"

"What do you mean?"

"Waka said there's a new student joining us in June."

"And you think it's Ai?"

"Might be." Fushimi took out her textbook right after.

Now I knew why everyone was so restless. It was impossible to not get excited about a new classmate.

Lunchtime.

I was having lunch in the physics room, all alone with Shizuka Torigoe, as usual.

Before I got back on good terms with Fushimi, she was the closest friend I had in school, and we had lunch together all the time in the quiet physics room. We didn't speak; we didn't even sit close together. It wasn't awkward, though. I found our time quite comfortable and relaxing.

"June, huh?" she said out of nowhere.

"What?"

"The new classmate."

"What's special about them coming in June?"

"There's a big event, remember?"

"…What was it, again?"

"The school field trip. I was just thinking about how they'll probably join us for that."

Right. I forgot because of all the talk about the school festival, but that was approaching soon, too.

The Japanese history teacher was away on a business trip, so we spent the period doing study hall.

Fushimi was smoothly writing across her worksheet.

"Even if the new person doesn't turn out to be Ai, it's pretty weird for someone to transfer in June, don't you think?" she suddenly asked.

"Well, not like it's normal to transfer schools in the first place."

My own worksheet was still blank. Hers was half done already. I tried taking a peek at her answers, but she blocked them with her arm.

"Ryou, no, look," she said, scolding me with a serious face. "Just check your textbook. The answers are all there."

She patiently explained the problems to me.

"Back to what I was saying—you'd change schools after summer break, like in September, wouldn't you? June's just weird."

"I thought so, too, but maybe they didn't want to miss the field trip."

In Torigoe's words, it was a "big event."

Study hall made it easy for conversations to spread around the classroom. They all started talking about the transfer student and the field trip, and people were already forming groups in anticipation.

The field trip can be exciting if you think of yourself as a tourist, visiting a distant place. But when you thought about it as a group activity for the whole class, or even school, it wasn't really the same.

During last year's trip, my group was a mishmash of all the people who couldn't join their friends due to the limit of people per group. Our room was awkward as hell, and they all went to see people in the other groups most of the time, so I basically stayed inside alone for a good chunk of the trip.

"How did Ai look?"

"Like a high school girl."

"Ha-ha-ha. Okay, sure, anything else?" Fushimi seemed to have found my answer hilarious.

"She was wearing a uniform I didn't recognize."

"Where did she move to, again?"

"I think it was Tokyo."

"Well, that's why you didn't recognize it."

Those who had already finished the worksheet went to talk with their friends. The seat before me was also empty now, and so Torigoe came, worksheet in hand.

"Shii, did you finish?"

"I'm almost done. You're already done, Hiina?"

"Hee-hee. Must I remind you I'm an honor student?"

This was unusual. Torigoe didn't usually come to us during study hall.

"Torigoe, whatcha come here for?"

"Ryou, don't be like that." Fushimi scowled at me. "We're all buddy-buddy. What other reason does she need?"

Buddy-buddy?? Who uses that unironically??

"N-no, it's not like I…" Torigoe turned red all the way to her ears, and her voice got quieter and quieter. "Anyway, that *buddy-buddy* thing sounds extremely dorky."

Fushimi froze. The implication that she was dorky had been increasingly sensitive for her lately, due to her poor taste in fashion. The comment only made it worse.

"I was just wondering what you two were planning," Torigoe said, facing away from us.

"Planning for what?"

"For the field trip."

Oh, so that's why she's here.

"Ryou, are you grouping with anyone else?"

If only I had a life where I could use the old "Sorry, I already agreed to join these other guys."

"Ryou, why are you looking away?"

"Just wondering about how things could've been in a parallel world."

"Huh?" Fushimi just blinked in confusion.

"Hey!" Torigoe turned around to us. "If you like… How about we… form a group together, all three of us, for the trip?"

Torigoe pouted in embarrassment, waiting for our reply.

How long had it been since I got asked to join something like this? It had been so long that it took me a while to process.

Fushimi, being her close friend, would surely agree right away…or so I thought. I glanced at her, but she was looking away, pensive. I was not expecting that reaction.

©Fly

"Do you already have plans with others?" I asked.

Fushimi shook her head. "No. Um, okay then, I'd be glad to."

Torigoe's expression brightened with relief.

"Good to know. But won't other people ask you to join their group, Hiina?"

"Ah."

I didn't know how many people were allowed in a group, but it had to be more than two.

"That just means we'll have to include some of Fushimi's other friends," I said.

They both chuckled.

"Looks like Ryou says yes, too."

"Yeah."

Hopefully, everything turns out well.

Fushimi and Torigoe then started talking about what to do during the trip.

I had to give props to Torigoe. It takes a lot of courage to ask someone to form a group with you. I knew exactly how hard that was.

Maybe it isn't a big deal to invite someone when you're confident in yourself or have always had a squad to hang out with. But for people without a lot of friends, we're always thinking thinks like, *They might say no* or *Maybe they don't even like me.* After seeing Torigoe working up the courage to ask us, it made me feel like I should be trying my best, too.

"Wonder which class Ai will end up in."

"Here, I guess. There's you and me," I replied.

"Ohh... I see. I can see that."

June was next week. The transfer student would be here soon.

I could have kept on calling her Ai, like we did as kids, but it would be too embarrassing. I decided to switch to a nickname instead.

"You two know the transfer student?"

"We still don't know if it's Himeji."

"There goes Ryou, trying to act like he doesn't care again."

"I am not."

"Just call her Ai like you always have."

"It's just embarrassing to keep talking the way we did as kids."

"Really?" Fushimi tilted her head. "So Ai transferred halfway through grade school. Ryou and I were friends with her," she explained to Torigoe.

Mana joined us often. I was the only boy among them, so the other guys always made fun of me for it.

"Oh, you were? Then…wouldn't that be a problem?" Torigoe frowned. "He meets his long-estranged childhood friend again… Reunited at the peak of adolescence, the distance between them closes…," she started narrating.

"Not happening." Fushimi shot it down. "*Not* happening," she repeated, more coldly this time.

Torigoe and I turned to look at her.

"Not happening," she said yet again.

Her cheeks were puffing up like a hamster's. She gloomily glanced down at the book in her hands.

"Takamori, do something," Torigoe hissed.

"No, you do it. Aren't you the one who's buddy-buddy with her?"

Torigoe chuckled.

"Don't laugh."

"How could I not?"

"Dorky, I know."

We were whispering to each other, but Fushimi still heard us.

"Oh, Hiina, are you reading the one I lent you?"

"Yeah. But I'm still at the beginning."

Oh, they started chatting. Or more like Torigoe managed to deflect the topic?

After parting ways with Fushimi, I went home. Mana was alrcady back, her loafers placed neatly at the entrance.

"What's for dinner tonight?"

I heard noises in the kitchen, so I peered in, and there she was: the *gyaru* in an apron. My sister, two years younger than me, was cutting something with a pleasant rhythm.

"Bubby, that shouldn't be the first thing to say after coming home."

What are you, my mother? Even she wouldn't say something like that.

"Okay. I'm home."

"Good to have you back." She grinned.

Your future husband will be so happy.

"Hey, do you remember Himeji... Ai?"

"Ai? You mean *that* Ai? I could never forget. We hung out together all the time." She took a sip of the miso soup she was making. "Oooh, that's good!" She nodded in satisfaction.

I didn't *forget* about her, either... I just didn't have any need to think about her—until I met her again, that is.

"Did you hear anything about her?"

"She's changing schools, right?"

So that part's true...

"How do you know that?"

"She has a brother my age, and I heard he's moving here. I just assumed she's coming, too."

"Oh." I huffed, acting uninterested.

I turned around to go watch TV in the living room, when the doorbell rang.

"Maybe that's Hina."

"Oh, I'll go get it." I stopped Mana as she was wiping her hands on the apron, and I walked toward the front door.

What could Fushimi possibly want?

The doorbell rang several more times, and that's when I realized it couldn't be her. She wouldn't do that.

"I'm coming!" I slipped on the sneakers I had just taken off and grabbed the doorknob.

"Good afternoon, Mr. Molester."

It was Himeji.

"Speak of the devil…"

Don't call me Mr. Molester, c'mon.

She was wearing the same uniform I saw that morning.

Her face was easily recognizable; she hadn't changed much from back then. Though when I looked closely, I saw she was wearing makeup now. But there was something different about her, from Fushimi or Torigoe. She looked more…sophisticated? Most guys would probably agree she was pretty.

"Hey, Himeji, did you need something?"

"What sort of a greeting is that? And uh… Himeji?" She stared at me, her eyes narrowed.

"You know, Himejima, Himeji? It rolls better off the tongue."

"Sure, I guess."

"So what do you want? I'm not a molester, just so you know. You ran off before I could explain what happened."

"I—I wasn't thinking. I just didn't want to make a scene."

If that's the case, don't pull me off the train in the first place.

"I'm here to tell you I'm transferring to the same school as you and Hina."

"Okay."

"Is that all you have to say? Can't you at least look happy about it?"

"Why?"

"Your childhood friend just came from far away to go to the same school as you again."

So?

She sure had some confidence to think I would have been excited to go to school with her again.

"We'll be in the same class, too," she said, puffing out her chest.

Apparently, she was on the train that morning to check out the route to school. She'd boarded at that station because she had gotten off there

©Fly

earlier to double-check she was on the right train. It was just bad luck that she ran into a groper.

"I even got to see the school and meet Miss Wakatabe."

"I'll tell you up front that I'm class rep, so please don't do anything weird."

"You? Ha-ha. Now that's good to know."

Why?

Himeji really was here just to say hi, it seemed. We kept on chatting, and the memories came back to me. She was the same as before, all the way to her mannerisms and way of speaking.

"Oh, right. Mana! Himeji's here," I shouted toward the kitchen. Immediately, I could hear her footsteps hurrying through the hallway.

"Wow, you're right! Ai!"

"Mana, long time no see."

"Longy!"

"Longy!"

What's that greeting? Short for "long time no see"?

"Bubby, why are you talking at the door? Let her in. Really, how many times do I have to teach you your manners?"

Maybe Mana grew up to be such a responsible person because I wasn't.

"You're right. So…are you gonna come in?" I asked her.

Himeji giggled. "You two are the same as always."

"And you've become such a city girl, Ai!"

"Oh, you turned into a full-fledged *gyaru*."

"Yup! Bubby just kept insisting, right?"

No, no. Why are you pulling me into this?

Himeji frowned, staring at me with palpable disgust in her eyes. "Why are you making your sister do this…?"

"I'm not. She got into the fashion scene all by herself. I never told her anything."

"No need to be embarrassed about it, Bubby."

"I am not."

What am I even supposed to be embarrassed about?

"Oh, right! Ai, would you like to stay for dinner? Where's your new house? Same as before?"

"Oh... I would love to, but you'll have to excuse me today. I only came to say hi, really."

"Awww."

Mom was going to come home late today, so having more people would've been great for Mana.

"I'll see you," Himeji said before turning around.

"Bye," I said, trying to close the door, but Mana stopped me.

"Bubby, walk her home."

"But it's not even that far."

"I'm sure you still have things to talk about, so go with her. She might not show it, but she gets lonely easily."

Was she that kinda girl?

I couldn't say no to Mana, so I put my sneakers back on and followed after Himeji.

"What do you want?" she snapped.

"I'm walking you home."

"It's right there, remember?"

Wow, she really did move back to the same house.

"Why did you transfer schools now? Pretty unusual timing, isn't it?"

"Is that bad?"

"No, I just wondered."

"What does it matter?"

I'll take that as there is actually a reason behind it.

"Tell Mana thanks for inviting me over for dinner. I just had mine prepared already."

"Got it. Come by when you can; I'm sure Mana would love it."

Just come only when she's there, too.

"Ryou, are you...?" She looked up at me, her head tilted to the side.

My heart skipped a beat. Even though she was my age, there was this charisma about her that made her feel like a college-age girl wearing a high school uniform.

"Am I…what?"

"Ha-ha, nothing."

Even though I knew her, her unfamiliar uniform and new air of maturity made her feel like a totally different person.

But despite her sophistication, her house was old-fashioned. It had been a while since I had seen it, but I was surprised at how dated it seemed.

"Thank you," she said before going inside, not looking back at me once.

Monday.

Just as she said, Himeji transferred into our class. She came in after Waka, and our homeroom teacher gave a simple introduction.

"This is Ai Himejima. She's transferring to our school today. You can ask her about her hobbies and what club she's joining and whatever later."

Everyone was whispering among themselves about how cute she was, wondering where that uniform was from.

She probably didn't have much time to prepare before moving; she was still wearing the uniform of her previous school.

Himeji didn't seem to have any interest in writing her name on the blackboard or introducing herself, either. She only said, "Nice to meet you" and bowed her head.

"Okay, everyone, welcome her," Waka said.

Everyone received her with applause.

Where will she sit, though?

"Oh. I forgot to prepare her desk," Waka muttered.

So the typical transfer student seat in the last row by the window side was missing because of her carelessness. Typical Waka.

"Now then, class reps, since Himejima is still unfamiliar with the school, make sure to look after her."

"All right," Fushimi answered.

"'Kay," I replied.

"Let's have her sit beside Takamori, so you can take good care of her."

Which one? The side where Fushimi is sitting or the boy next to me?

"Oh, I'll move," the guy said.

Waka took him up on his offer, and he gave up his seat. I was then told to get another desk to place in the last row for him later. Himeji took the seat beside me, opposite from Fushimi.

"Must be hard being a class rep, huh?" she whispered without glancing at me. She took a notebook out of her bag as everyone stared at her.

I whispered back, "I'm basically a handyman. There's a lot to do, but it's mostly behind-the-scenes stuff, so it's actually easier than what you'd do in an event-related committee."

"Is that so?"

Then I felt a piercing stare from the other side.

"…" I turned and found Fushimi looking at me with eyes like an abandoned puppy's. "What happened?"

"Nothing…"

Doesn't look like nothing.

Waka spoke before I could say anything else. "Give her a tour around the school once you get the time. It can be either of you or both, okay? All right, homeroom's over." She grabbed the attendance sheet and left the classroom.

"Oh, don't worry about the tour," Himeji said. "Unless there's something cool I wouldn't find otherwise."

"No, she asked us to," Fushimi answered in earnest.

Himeji tried to say something back, but before she could, a crowd gathered around her. It happened in an instant; everyone was curious about the pretty new student.

Even people from the next class over came to take a look at her. The panda-at-the-zoo effect wouldn't wear off for a little while.

"Fushimi, what do you wanna do about the school tour?"

"Let's do it together."

Our school didn't really have any unique spots besides the special classrooms building, the gym, and the cafeteria. And she didn't even want a tour.

So I got up from my seat and took the opportunity to go grab that desk Waka told me to get.

"Takamori, I'll help you out," Torigoe said.

She followed me just for that?

"Thanks."

I gave her the chair, and she sighed.

"What's up?"

"Oh, sorry… I was thinking this new girl is really amazing."

"Amazing?"

"Yeah, it's like she's sparkling? She has this very strong positive vibe."

I think I know what you mean.

Using Torigoe's language, I was probably emitting "negative vibes." And she was, too, probably.

On our way back to the classroom, Fushimi showed up and hurried toward us.

"I'll help, too."

Nice of both of them to help me out with my job.

"Hiina, is Himejima also your childhood friend?"

"More like she just spent half of grade school with us… That doesn't really count, does it? Does it?"

Why twice?

"Does it not?" I said. "We were together all the time from preschool up to her move… And the same thing kinda happened with you? I think we can call her our childhood friend."

"So he says, Hiina. Any thoughts?" Torigoe insisted, like she was interviewing her.

"No. She doesn't count."

Why did she use such a definitive tone?

"I mean, it's not like you can only have one childhood friend, right?" Torigoe said.

Fushimi couldn't argue back.

"One is enough." She pouted.

"So she says, Takamori. What do you think?"

What are you trying to do here?

"Himeji, what're you planning to do for lunch?"

I asked her before class started; after all, we'd been told to take care of her.

"Do you want to spend it with me?" she replied.

"That's not what I'm asking."

"Do you eat lunch alone all the time or something, Ryou?" she asked with a mocking smile.

"I do not, actually. But I thought you might not have anyone."

"Uh-huh." She grinned; I turned my head. "Sure, I can grace you with my presence for lunch."

What's with the condescending tone?

Apparently, she had already been invited by other groups.

"I'm just asking you because that'd be the best time to show you around the school."

She giggled. "Yeah, let's go with that."

What the heck are you trying to imply?

"Ai, Ryou only asked you as class rep. As part of his job."

"Yeah, you wish, Hina."

"It's the truth!"

Can you guys not argue with me here, please?

"Ryou is more diligent than you expect. He always does what Waka tells him to."

"Sure, it's fine. Whatever. No need to get so worked up over it." Fushimi fiercely glared at her.

"I see you're still acting like a good girl, Hina."

"What's that supposed to mean?"

"Exactly what it sounds like."

Come to think of it, Himeji and I argued occasionally back then. As did Fushimi and I. But by far, the most arguments were fought between…

"I see you're still acting like you're just too cool to care 'cause you know everything."

"…" Himeji said nothing back, but I could feel she was slowly getting angrier.

These were the stereotypical childhood friends—they got along so well they argued all the time.

Yeah, this is what it was like back then.

As I soaked in nostalgia, things kept on heating up between them.

"But it's okay; I'll still give you that tour."

"I don't want a tour from anyone with that attitude."

Okay, Himeji, but what about your attitude?

Fushimi scowled at me. "You hear that, Ryou? She doesn't want a tour."

She did say the same thing when I asked her.

"I guess we don't have to, then," I said.

"Hold up. I didn't say I didn't want it."

Make up your mind.

"I just didn't want to take up your time since you seem so busy with your class rep work, Ryou…," Himeji whispered.

Oh. Guess it's my fault for saying I had lots to do.

"Yes, Ryou is super busy. He's got tons of studying to do, too, so he has no time for you."

Crap. I forgot about that. I have another study session with Professor Hina after school today.

"Hina, what are you to him? Why are you deciding everything for him?"

"I'm his childhood friend; is that a problem?!"

"I'm his, too."

Fushimi looked just about ready to literally bark at her, while Himeji's sidelong glance was shooting daggers.

Why can't you two get along for two seconds? You finally meet again after such a long time.

The teacher then came in, and although I rarely led the class greeting, I decided to do it this time. Luckily, this put a stop to their fight.

When I thought about it, Himeji was about the only person who could get Fushimi so worked up—now that was proof of their long-lasting friendship.

Lunchtime came, and a group of girls immediately surrounded Himeji. She gave me one regretful glance before joining the girls' conversation with ease.

She really stood out—not only due to her uniform but also because of her looks. Boys from other classes also came by to check her out.

It looked like she would fit right in with the rest of the class, so there was no need for Fushimi or me to be particularly concerned.

Just as I was sighing in relief, another classmate came for Fushimi, half forcing her to go to the cafeteria.

"Ryou, let's talk later!" She waved at me, disappearing into the crowd in the hallway.

Once that was settled, I decided to spend my lunchtime in quiet as always.

I arrived at my precious lunch spot. Torigoe glanced at me once I entered, but she immediately looked back at her phone.

"Himejima's pretty popular, huh?"

"Transfer students always are."

Though in this case, her looks definitely added to her popularity.

I sat down in my usual seat with an awkward smile.

I opened the lunch box that Mana made for me and dug in.

What was happening to Himeji now was pretty much exactly what happened to Fushimi at the start of middle school and high school.

"I didn't expect her to be like that."

"What do you mean?" I asked her.

"Nothing." Torigoe shook her head. "But we may have a three-way struggle on our hands…" She kept on grumbling to herself. "I need a new strategy… Hmmm…" She crossed her arms, looking pensive. "Hey, which one did you like more?"

"What?"

"Between Hiina and Himejima. You guys were close, right?"

"Yeah, we were, but…"

Thinking back on it, maybe there was something there.

"Kids are simple. They think hanging out with someone is the same as loving them—and end up thinking they have those feelings for them," Torigoe said.

We did hang out a lot, and I had a lot of fun with them, so I liked them in that way. Makes sense. I guess there's no need for me to mull over the meaning of love when she puts it that simply.

"So I was wondering if maybe you liked one of them," she continued.

"Even if I did, it doesn't mean I still do."

"Yeah… But I know someone who still has those elementary-school feelings, so I thought I'd ask."

You actually know someone that devoted?

"Weren't you going to show this Himeji girl around school?"

"That was the plan, but she's too busy for that now…"

Just as I was saying that, the door to the physics room opened with a thud.

"There you are. What are you doing here just chilling without me?"

Speak of the devil again. Himeji was frowning, hands on her hips.

"I didn't leave you behind... And it doesn't have to be me giving the tour; I'm sure someone else will gladly do it for you."

"Give me that tour. It's your job, isn't it?"

Unfortunately, I don't have Fushimi's ability to argue back.

I asked how she found out I was here, and then she said she saw me go in.

Right. This room is basically facing our classroom.

I finished my lunch and left the room as she asked.

"There's nothing special here, really," I warned her.

We started with the special classrooms building, then the teachers' lounge. I pointed out the clubrooms building from the window, and then we went to the cafeteria.

"Pretty normal."

"I told you."

As we walked down the hallways, everyone's eyes were drawn to Himeji.

I told her the location of the sports grounds and finished the tour by showing her the gym. Guys in T-shirts and their uniform slacks were playing basketball inside.

"This is the gym. Very normal."

"Yup. That's a gym, all right."

"Well, it is a typical school."

The school curriculum was general, too. We could only choose between science or art electives after summer break in our second year. Nothing special.

"Remember when we hung out in the gym storage room in grade school?" she said.

"In the storage room?"

That was a typical place for grade-schoolers to play around, but I couldn't remember specifically doing that with Himeji.

She sighed, then slowly entered the warehouse.

I followed her and saw her looking around for something.

"Oh, there it is." She found a high jump landing mat and sat down on it. Her body weight softly pushed it down. "You really don't remember at all?"

"I mean, it's not like I forgot everything, but…"

She tapped the spot beside her, and I sat down.

We could hear the boys' voices and the ball's bouncing from outside the storage room.

"I remember it all," she mused.

"Really?"

"It was all so fun, before I moved."

As kids, we could play around without worrying about anything. Nowadays, just asking a girl to hang out is so complicated—you have to think about whether you like her *that* way, and it becomes a mental tug-of-war.

"Please try to get along with Fushimi," I said.

"Why? I mean, why do you ask that?"

"Because it doesn't feel good being caught in the middle of your arguments."

"Ah-ha-ha. I think we were always arguing, though."

"I mean, yeah, but can't you guys act a bit more mature?"

You're not grade-schoolers anymore.

"As far as I can tell, I'm still me, and she's still her. That's why we clash like that, I think. But…"

She pulled my necktie. Her face got close to mine, and as soon as my heart skipped a beat, she pushed me down. It happened so suddenly that I couldn't even react in time. I lay on my back on the mat, and she placed her hands beside my ears.

"Do you have anything to say?" she asked in a provocative tone, staring deep into my eyes.

"Yeah. What the hell are you doing?"

"You still don't remember?"

Remember what?

Then a smile escaped her. "I'll give you a warning. Don't think I still like you, Ryou. It's not gonna be that easy."

Still? So then…

"You mean you liked me back then?"

She kept quiet with a serious expression. Then she realized she slipped up and started getting redder and redder.

"You… I—I told you so, so many times… Why won't this stupid guy remember?"

She slapped my chest.

"Yeah… I get that a lot. Sorry."

"Whatever. It's all in the past," she said quickly.

A guy came to return a basketball, but he didn't come inside, just softly rolled the ball over. Basically saying "*You guys can put it away.*"

"Himeji, we should go."

"Have you kissed someone else already?"

"Huh?"

Fushimi's face flashed in my mind. At the same time, I wondered why she asked.

"No… Forget I asked that."

"Ryou, Ryou."

Classes were over. We were studying in the library. Fushimi was sitting at the other side of the table.

"Huh? Uh, what's up?"

"You've been lost in thought this whole time. What happened?"

"Nothing."

"Then pay more attention," Professor Hina said before explaining the problem again.

At the counter near the entrance was Torigoe, doing her important librarian duties of reading a thick hardcover book.

Why did Himeji say that at the gym...?

"Was Himeji always like that?"

"I think so. At least from my point of view, she seems the same as before."

"Maybe more mature now."

"I mean, yeah, she's a high schooler." She stared at me, then brushed her hair to the side, gently holding her other arm.

"What's wrong? You seem anxious."

"I'm more mature now, too."

It was hard noticing any small changes since I saw her every day. Maybe I would've noticed if we hadn't seen each other in forever, like with Himeji.

Fushimi looked gloomily to the side, then stroked her glossy lips with a finger. I could tell she was trying to act more mature.

"That's not really what Himeji's like, though," I said.

"She is!"

Himeji's more like... Oh, I know.

I finally realized how she was different from Fushimi.

She was more voluptuous.

"Ryou," Fushimi said, narrowing her eyes and scolding me like a mischievous puppy. "Are you having dirty thoughts?"

"No. What do you mean?"

"Y-you know what I mean! Obscene thoughts! Dirty ideas! Forget it!" She tried to change the conversation, her face red.

Torigoe glanced at us in reaction to Fushimi's shouting, then sighed before looking back at her book.

"Hiina, keep it down."

"Sorry. But it's Ryou's fault."

"Yeah, I was listening."

"Then you should know it's *not* my fault, right?" I said.

"Maybe. You didn't say anything. But I also saw that look you gave her."

There were only a couple people there besides us, but we had to whisper if we didn't want to be heard.

Fushimi cleared her throat and instructed me to go back to my assignment.

I grabbed my pencil, glanced at problem number one, and immediately murmured, "Hey, Fushimi."

"Hmm? Stumped already?" she asked, her voice as low as mine.

"No, it's not about that."

I remembered what Himeji had asked at the gym storage room. And I realized that I'd never properly talked with Fushimi about the *incident* since it happened.

"You know how we went barbecuing in the mountains and did fireworks. I wanted to talk about that."

©Fly

"Ah! Huh?! You're bringing that up *here*?" She started panicking. "Um, uh, give me a moment."

She placed her workbook beside her face. Hiding behind it and leaning in close would make it at least harder for others to hear. I grabbed my workbook and did the same.

"…"

Her face was way closer than I expected.

Her cheeks grew red, and she looked away.

"Th-this is pretty embarrassing."

"Y-yeah."

We were still whispering.

"So I wanna ask… Is it okay to kiss without going out?"

"Huh?" She opened her eyes wide. "N-not like it's a crime… So I think it's okay?"

"I see. Okay, then."

"Ryou, I think your sense of virtue is a few centuries behind…"

I just thought these things had a proper order to them, y'know? But if it's okay with you, then cool.

"I—I mean… Kisses are…an expression of love," she said, her face getting redder as she flipped quickly through the workbook's pages. "B-but I guess I got carried away… I wish the mood was a little more appropriate for it."

She got to the last page, then flipped back to the beginning and restarted it all. Her eyes were swirling around like they do in comics as she went through her second round of flipping pages.

"My head's hurting now; I'm feeling sick…"

From thinking too much?

"Are you okay?" I asked.

"Oh, I'm fine." She covered her face with a handkerchief. "It's just—I basically forced you to do it, so I thought I should apologize."

"You don't have to; don't worry."

I was about to add "I'm *not worried about it*," but then it would sound like I was pretending it never happened.

I was shocked and frozen in place when it happened, partly due to how sudden it was and partly because, well, it was a kiss. My reaction was pretty silly, to be honest.

Fushimi put her handkerchief away and let her gaze fall.

"I'm not as much of a good girl as you think."

"Well, not like you're a bad one, either."

"No, I am. I was being underhanded then."

...Underhanded?

She looked away, to Torigoe, but she quickly turned to face me again.

"But I won't ever tell you to forget about it." Fushimi's voice was firm. "Have you ever wanted to kiss?"

"Wait, where's this coming from?"

"I have."

She looked straight at me, her face red to the ears. The scent of her shampoo reached my nose.

Up until it happened, I had only imagined what a kiss would feel like. It was over in the blink of an eye, but still, that sensation lingered in my mind.

I had to force myself to not look at her lips.

Fushimi could no longer handle the silence, and she covered her face with both hands, then laid her face on the desk.

"F-forget what I just said." She swung her feet back and forth.

"Stop flirting in the library," the librarian warned us with an icy tone.

"We are not flirting," I replied.

Fushimi giggled. "We got in trouble."

I could only sigh.

3) The Three Childhood Friends

◆Mana Takamori◆

Mana arrived at her usual supermarket and looked at the flyer posted outside the store.

"Hmmm, so frozen foods are on sale today."

She took out her phone and opened a social media app. Her objective was not checking out celebrities' posts or the number of likes on her own—she was looking up another supermarket in the neighborhood.

She found someone who had posted that the prices at the other store weren't as cheap.

Mana grabbed a basket and entered the supermarket, and she came across Hina in the produce aisle.

"Hina!"

"Oh, Mana. Hi!"

"'Sup! Whatcha doin'?"

"I got asked to do some shopping."

Hina's awkward smile was adorable. Mana thought about how she would be attending the same school as her next year—but then she remembered that her homeroom teacher had asked her to aim for a better one, since she had the grades.

"You're not with Bubby?"

"We just said good-bye to each other, actually."

That meant her brother was likely at home already. Probably chilling in his room with a cup of juice.

They chatted as they shopped together. Mana also grabbed some extra snacks for her brother, since she had enough left in the food budget her mother gave her. Then Hina told her about their other childhood friend who had just come back, Ai Himejima.

"So you're all back together now!"

"Yeah, but…"

Mana saw that Hina wasn't as excited. "Hina, are you worried about her? Think she's gonna take Bubby away from you?"

"Ah… N-no."

She totally was. But that was also a good thing about her: She was easy to read.

"Suuure," Mana replied with a warm expression, and she didn't pry further. "Hey, what do you like about Bubby?"

"Huh?"

"I was just wondering what you see in him."

"Well, that's…you know," Hina replied, flustered.

"C'mon, no need to hide anything with me." Mana kept poking at Hina, who eventually caved in.

"I feel safe with Ryou."

"Oh, I get that." Mana nodded deeply. "Is that the only reason?"

He wasn't smart or athletic, which was what usually made middle and high schoolers popular (although looks were generally most important). Hina's choice to prioritize a sense of security just showed how sophisticated her tastes were relative to her peers.

"I mean, Ryou doesn't seem to be interested in *anything*. And that's what's good about him."

"It is?" Mana chuckled.

"To me, at least." Fushimi beamed.

Her smile was a perfect example of one of the aforementioned popularity factors—it even made Mana's heart skip a beat.

"After grade school, everyone was coming to me all the time for everything—always trying to talk with me, even after class. They never left me alone."

She reminisced about her time in middle school. Soon after school started, everyone in school, boys and girls, was talking about how pretty she was.

"I guess that's not news to Bubby at all."

"He hasn't changed in the slightest, really. No matter how I look or how popular I am, he still treats me the same way he did back then."

And that sense of security comforted her.

"He's so dense, and since he doesn't try to stick his nose into my business, it makes me want to poke mine into his." She grinned, as though recalling something.

"I think most boys around the world would shed tears of joy if they heard that."

Mana could only picture her own brother grimacing in response.

The two girls lined up at different registers. Mana paid for her items and bagged her groceries in reusable bags.

"Mana, you're so conscientious…"

"Why?"

"Those bags…"

"Oh yeah, I mean, why would I want the plastic ones anyway? You just end up throwing them out, so it's better to just use these."

Hina gasped in admiration, so floored she stopped packing her own items.

"But you're a *gyaru*."

"*Gyarus* are good." Mana grinned, then hung her bag from her shoulder and exited the store.

They walked back home together, and halfway through, they came across the third childhood friend.

"Oh, Ai! It's been a minute!"

"Sure has."

Ai walked toward them, waving. She was attractive, too, though in a different way than Hina. Mana's eyes were glued to her.

"Do I have something on my face?"

"No, I was just amazed at how much you've grown. In all sorts of ways."

"What?" Ai laughed. "Same goes for you, though."

Hina was purer and more innocent, whereas Ai was more refined. They were like a sunflower and a rose.

"Ai, I heard Ryou showed you around school."

"He did. I considered asking you, too, but you seemed busy."

"Ugh." Hina couldn't say anything else in response.

"Must be hard having such a big fan base."

"They're not like that all the time. I spend lunchtime with Ryou sometimes, too."

"Okay. I just asked him because he seemed like he had nothing better to do."

"I see."

Mana could tell Hina was relieved at hearing Ai had no ulterior motives.

They walked together for a while, until Mana remembered a bit of their past and giggled.

"Remember when you two fought over who would get to marry Bubby?"

Hina's shoulders tensed.

"That was when we were in second grade, right?" Ai replied much more calmly.

"Yeah. I was still in preschool, so that must be it."

"I remember that. Hina started bawling her eyes out, and we didn't know what to do."

"Ah-ha-ha. Yeah, that happened."

"N-no, that was just because Ai kept insisting that Ryou said he liked her."

"I don't remember that."

"Aw, really! You only remember things that conveniently won't embarrass you!"

"I'm sure you started crying because you thought that would solve things."

"Here we go again." Mana looked at them, feeling nostalgic. "This really takes me back. I think I eventually said I would marry him, and then there would be no need to fight. And that was that."

""That did not happen.""

Oops, they do remember.

Mana looked away, sticking out her tongue.

They didn't usually argue that much, but almost every time they did, her brother was the cause.

"Hey, let's throw a welcome-back party for Ai!"

"That sounds great!" Hina immediately agreed. She might have argued with Ai a lot, but she held no ill will against her.

"N-no, it's fine. I don't want to…take up your time…"

"Aw, still so shy."

"Riiight?"

"Sh-shut it! I just don't like that sort of thing," Ai muttered, averting her eyes.

Mana and Hina turned to look at each other and smiled.

It was so nice to know some things were always the same.

©Fly

4 The Last Boy to Join a Team

Himeji was still as popular as ever during break times. I went to the restroom for a bit, and she was surrounded by people by the time I came back.

"Must be tiring, huh, Ryou?" Fushimi commented.

"You know, this is what it felt like when I was assigned the seat next to yours."

"Huh? Really?"

She didn't seem to remember what it was like.

"Hey, Himejima," said one of the classmates around her. "I heard…"

"You were at the gym storeroom yesterday?"

"Who was the boy?"

The topic had been brought up all day since the morning.

Yeah, that guy totally saw her pinning me down…

And the pretty new girl in a unique uniform was hard to miss.

On her first day, the transfer student was seen pinning down a boy in the gym storage room. It was certainly exciting news in the midst of our peaceful, boring student lives.

"Did something happen to Ai yesterday?" Fushimi asked me.

I couldn't tell her the truth. Thankfully, the rumors didn't seem to name me as the boy in question, so I decided to feign ignorance.

"Dunno," I replied, expressionless.

"What do you mean you 'dunno'?" Himeji said from beyond the crowd.

Isn't your hearing a bit too good?!

"Ryou?" Himeji called again.

"..."

I could feel a piercing stare on my back.

"What? Are you two hiding something?"

I turned back to look at Fushimi, and she was clearly upset.

"No, I mean... It was nothing."

"So that was nothing to you, Ryou? When did you get to be such a Casanova?" Himeji was grinning broadly.

What am I supposed to say here...?

"Don't leave me out." Fushimi's voice sounded sad.

"See? Now Fushimi's sad because of you."

"What did I do? You're always taking her side."

Please stop already...

Everyone surrounding Himeji was now looking at us.

"So you're friends with Fushimi and the prez, Himejima?"

"We were always together up until I moved away during grade school."

Everyone accepted Himeji's explanation without question.

Although things were a bit awkward yesterday, I was able to talk with Himeji like normal. Apparently, it was the same for Fushimi.

When Waka came into the classroom, the people surrounding Himeji all went back to their own seats and classrooms.

The last class for the day was homeroom.

I thought we'd talk about the film for the festival, but the topic turned out to be that other event Torigoe mentioned.

"Seems like you've decided to make your own short film for the school festival. I thought you wouldn't make up your mind, and we'd have to do it during our field trip on the bus. Ah-ha-ha!" Waka said.

Hey. Were you planning on bringing down the mood of our (hopefully) fun trip with that?

"Other classes haven't made up their minds yet, so I guess we're ahead of the curve. I'm proud of you guys!"

Waka glanced at Fushimi and me. I was a little embarrassed.

"To get you up to speed, Himejima, the class has decided to film a movie for the school festival in the fall. I know this plan was made without your input, but please help them out."

"Yes, of course," Himeji answered.

We already decided Fushimi would have the leading role, thanks to both her looks and her theater studies, but perhaps things wouldn't have been as clear-cut had Himeji been present back then.

I took out a crumpled-up piece of paper from my desk—the one Fushimi had prepared for her presentation, which explained the process of the making of the film.

"Wow," Himeji exclaimed. She was looking at my hands. "You have it all well thought out."

"Yeah. We want to make a good movie, not just some cheap kiddie project."

"Sounds good."

She was more receptive to the idea than I expected. Since she looked interested, I gave her the wrinkly piece of paper. I could always just ask Fushimi later if I needed something.

Himeji stared intently at Fushimi's handwritten plan.

"Did Hina make this?"

"Yup. How could you tell?"

"Her handwriting hasn't changed much since then. Wait, is this the only one?"

"It is," I replied bluntly.

While we were chatting, pamphlets of the trip were handed out to the class.

I grabbed my copy and passed the rest behind.

I first looked at the place and dates. Two nights and three days. The schedule was pretty much what you'd expect of a touristy trip.

"Can't wait for it, huh, Ryou?" Fushimi said.

Everyone started talking about the trip, so Waka had to clap twice to get their attention.

"Okay, okay, quiet down. As you can tell from the schedule, you have some free time with your groups, so let's decide those now. These should consist of about five or six people. Decide on a group leader and make a schedule for the aforementioned free time…"

Five or six people…

I always hated whenever the teacher told us to make groups, but fortunately, Torigoe had already asked us. We three were set in stone… Right?

I turned around to glance at Silent Beauty Torigoe; her face was tense. Maybe she was worried whether we'd really form the group, even after she asked us.

"Go make those groups," Waka said, and everyone stood up and started forming groups.

"All right." Fushimi scooted her desk over to mine, and Torigoe walked to the seat in front of my desk, which was already empty.

We looked at each other and nodded.

"What about you, Ai?"

Surprisingly, no one went to ask Himeji to join. They might've been interested in the transfer student, but that didn't mean they would allow her into their group of friends.

"You want me to? I thought you'd be the last one to ask, Hina."

"Of course not," Fushimi replied with a smile.

"Join us, Himeji," Torigoe added.

I had to give her another push, then. "C'mon, Himeji. Otherwise, you'll end up wherever the teacher places you."

"You all like me, huh…," she muttered, hiding her embarrassment by playing with her hair.

"I do like you, Ai," said Fushimi.

"Don't say that!"

"Do you like me?"

"I— No!"

Fushimi grinned. She clearly knew how to handle her.

"What about you, Torigoe? What do you think of Himeji?" I asked.

"Huh? I don't know. But that just makes me want to find out."

Very Torigoe-ish response.

I looked around and saw that most groups had already been created. There were some noisy mixed-gender groups, some club-only groups, other groups of girls or boys only and such.

"I thought some other boy would come join us, but I guess not."

"Even if someone tried, the ulterior motive would be really obvious, so good thing that didn't happen," Fushimi said, with very good reason.

"If someone tried to befriend us now, they would have to either be the bravest or the stupidest guy in the world," Himeji said in agreement. "Our guards are up now."

But still, our group only had four people. We needed one or two more members.

I looked around searching for someone, when I saw a guy who had been left out.

"Crap… Everyone's in a group already." He ran his fingers through his hair.

Yup. He was sleeping in class. He had an obvious mark from it on his face.

It was the guy I thought I might get along with back during the meeting for the school festival.

"Hey, mind if I invite him?"

"No, go ahead," Fushimi said. Torigoe and Himeji also nodded.

…And now I'm getting nervous.

"…His name is Deguchi," Torigoe whispered to me.

Thank you.

"H-hey… Deguchi. Wanna join us?"

"Huh? Really? Agh! It's a group full of pretty girls! You sure you want *me* to join?"

Despite his claims, he still walked over to us. The guy had foxlike eyes and didn't appear to be in any club.

He sat down on the chair in front of Fushimi's, with the backrest in front.

"Well, now that I've been scouted by Takamori, I gotta join. Nice to meet ya."

Everyone greeted him as well.

"You saved me there. It would've been so awkward getting chucked into a bunch of randos."

Deguchi seemed honestly grateful.

Yeah, I had the feeling I could become friends with this guy.

Schedule sheets were handed out to each group, and Fushimi was to fill it out as our representative.

We had to visit some temples and places decided by the school, but we could choose the order and times on our own.

"First, let's go here."

Himeji, Torigoe, and Fushimi stared intently at the map. Deguchi and I had no room to butt in. Like, physically, no room—the girls were squeezed next to each other. I thought about opening the map app on my phone, but they were technically not allowed in school, so I decided against it.

Deguchi watched the girls talking.

"No room for us guys in the planning stages, huh?"

"Y-yeah…"

I wasn't sure how to talk with him. *Just be normal*, I thought… But what is "normal" to me anyway?

"Oh well. Not like I have anywhere I want to go to." He chuckled to himself.

"What class were you in last year?" I asked.

"A," he answered.

"Oh."

I knew no one from that class, so the conversation ended there.

Maybe…I'm just not good at talking to people?

Torigoe glanced at us, then looked back at the map. "Takamori's acting weird."

"Ryou?" said Fushimi.

"He's always weird."

I can hear you, Himeji.

"He's talking to Deguchi."

"I thought he didn't care about anyone in our class!" Fushimi turned to look at me.

Her eyes were brimming with expectation and endearment, like a mother watching her baby stand up for the first time.

Stop looking at me like that. I'm not your son.

"Hey, Takamori, your class was running a café at last year's school festival, right?"

"Huh? How did you know?"

"I went to take a look at Fushimi and saw this guy working so earnestly. It left an impression."

Yeah, I was, though was that really enough to leave an impression?

As Deguchi said, I was working at the café at last year's school festival; just doing what I was told to, really. And I had to keep it up even after my shift ended because the classmate who was supposed to switch with me never came back.

I explained that to him, and Deguchi laughed out loud. "I would've bailed, dude."

"I thought about it, but there was someone else working hard there, too." I glanced at the girl in question as I spoke.

"H-here! It was around here, that fancy tart shop!" Fushimi enthusiastically explained why the shop was so famous.

Fushimi and I were still basically estranged during that festival.

She was also working diligently back then, turning down her friends' invitations as she covered for the classmate who wouldn't come back to take over her shift.

"And I had nothing else to do even if I bailed, so," I added with an awkward smile. "By the way, I hope you're cool with me talking to you so casually."

"It's cool. I appreciate it."

Was that a weird thing to say?

I rarely came up to people like that; I wasn't sure how to become familiar with someone naturally.

"Did you hear that?" Fushimi gushed. "Awww, they're becoming friends."

"He's actually trying to speak with the guy," Torigoe said.

"Is that weird?" Himeji asked.

""For him, yes.""

You guys, stop commenting on it. You're only making things awkward for me.

"Oh, right. Ryou, we want to go to a tart shop. Is that okay with you? And Deguchi, too?" Fushimi asked.

We both gave confirmation, and she immediately turned back to the other girls.

"Just now, you said you went to our café for Fushimi. What did you mean by that?"

"I just heard the prettiest girl in school was there, so I had to take a look. Any guy would do the same, right?"

Unfortunately for him, we weren't using costumes of any kind—we had the same getup you'd usually wear for cooking class: dull apron, face mask, and headcloth.

"Due to the masks, I couldn't even tell which of them was Fushimi."

"Oh, really?"

"If you had done a cosplay café, I'm sure you would've had tons of people coming. Could've even charged for entry."

That would have been fine if she only had to be a waitress, but we had to work behind the counter preparing food and drinks, too. We probably disappointed a lot of people just like him.

As the girls continued excitedly planning the trip, Deguchi lowered his voice:

"…Takamori, I know you and Fushimi have been friends for a long time, but don't you think you're a little *too* chummy?"

"You think so? Not gonna say we're on bad terms or anything, but I don't feel like we're *that* close…"

What even is the appropriate distance between childhood friends?

We commuted to and from school together, helped each other out in class rep work, and sometimes hung out at each other's house. That was pretty much exactly the definition of what "friends" was to me.

There was the kiss thing, but that was outside my control, and I definitely had no idea how to take it. Fushimi had wanted to apologize for it.

"Aren't you two dating, actually?" he asked.

I had a coughing fit after hearing that. "Where'd you get that idea from?"

"That's kinda how it looks. Other childhood friends I know don't get along like you two. And we're talking about a guy and girl here, y'know. Makes you wonder." He paused. "Sorry. Yeah, it's weird how we start assuming romance just by seeing a guy and a girl hang out together in school."

Seriously. You have two people who get along, and everyone comes pouring out of the woodwork to say they're in love. That was school life for you.

"Guess I should ask. Are you gay?"

Deguchi's dead-serious expression as he asked that had me almost laughing.

There was someone else who didn't take it as lightly, though. I noticed Torigoe's head turning over here, her expression a blend of hope and worry.

"No." I was sure of that much.

"Look, they're talking about love," said Fushimi.

"Yeah, and they're serious about it," added Torigoe.

"Leave them alone," said Himeji. "Ryou's a teenage boy."

Why are they so fascinated by our conversation?

The schedule was done before I knew it. Fushimi outlined the details, and we all agreed on its contents. We submitted it to Waka and were allowed to leave school.

On our way back home, Fushimi asked:

"What would you do if Deguchi told you he liked me?"

"What?"

Was she listening to our entire conversation? A similar question had come up then.

If Deguchi liked her, huh…, I pondered.

"I would think he's just jumping on the bandwagon."

"Huh? That's it?" She puffed her cheeks. "Don't you think having a friend who likes the same person as you would cause problems? It's not weird to ask them outright if you suspect that might be the case."

Does that mean Deguchi suspected me?

"All the guys would turn against me if they thought I liked you."

"And yet you've defeated each and every one of them up to now."

"I don't remember winning any fights."

"You just don't notice. You're too dense."

"What?"

"Ha-ha-ha, you're just like the protagonist of this web novel where…" She didn't stop until she had merrily explained the whole series.

"I might be making a friend." I told Shinohara the highlight of my day through the phone.

"...*Why are you telling me this?*"

Shinohara sounded annoyed. It wasn't even that late. Was she mad I still had her manga?

"Mana's reading your book now; let me borrow it for a bit longer."

"*That's not what I asked.*" She sighed. "*Good for you, you're becoming friends with the guy in your group.*"

"This might be my last chance to make a guy friend."

"*Why are you so nervous about it?*"

Because I have no other friends.

"Remember what you said back at our barbecue? It seems I could get along with him, and I don't want him to hate me now. You know how that feels."

"*Ah...*" She sounded like she remembered. "*So, Takaryou, are you gay?*"

"I am not."

Both Shinohara and Torigoe liked when Bs fell in L so I could understand their reaction, but why does everyone automatically assume it's romantic whenever I try to get along with anyone?

"You know how there's stuff girls can only talk with other girls about, right? It's the same for guys."

"*I guess.*"

I always wanted to have those kinds of conversations you can only do with guys. I heard them around the classroom all the time. They weren't the kind of topics I could just casually talk about with Fushimi or Torigoe or Himeji.

Maybe it's mostly dirty jokes and other nonsense, but I didn't really see it that way. That stuff isn't as worthless as you might think.

"*You're so awkward, Takaryou. The more I talk to you, the more painfully obvious it is. You have no guts. It's a bit of a pain.*"

"Okay, that hurts to hear, you know?"

"*Ah-ha-ha-ha,*" she cackled. "*Sorry. You may be insensitive and dense, but you know, in a good way.*"

"O-okay...?"

"*I guess you have your delicate and sensible side, too. That's a good thing.*"

I don't know whether she's still insulting me, or...

"*Whenever I get the feeling you might be able to actually take a hint, it turns out you can't. But that's fine.*"

...No, yeah, she totally is.

"You can't just bad-mouth me and add 'That's a good thing' at the end and expect me to be happy about it."

She giggled, as though she was expecting that answer, then sighed.

"*Why do you talk to me about this sort of thing?*"

"You kinda feel like the big sister."

"*Really?*"

"Perhaps that's impossible to imagine when thinking about your dark past in middle school, but—"

"*Okay, never mention that again. Got it?*"

I felt chills down my spine.

"Let me finish. As I was saying—you're kind, Shinohara. I just feel I can have a calm and collected conversation with you."

"*Stop trying to butter me up... Now I'm feeling bad about insulting you.*"

Then don't?

"See? That's the kind of imposing competency I'm talking about, Boss."

"And stop trying to make that nickname a thing. Seriously."

I stopped the jokes; she was starting to sound really angry.

In the end, she advised me to just make small talk with the guy. I argued back, saying *that* was why the whole thing was hard, but she said we had the field trip to talk about and should go from there. Such wisdom.

Mana came into my room as soon as I hung up. *Was she waiting for that?*

"Bubby, who were you talking to? Hina?"

"Why do you care?"

"I just do! Please!"

I asked why.

"Don't eavesdrop. And knock before you come in."

"Hmmm, but if I did knock…"

"Then what?"

"Then you wouldn't get mad."

And that's a bad thing?

"That would be no fun."

"Don't use my reactions for your entertainment."

"Don't you get that this is how I express my love?"

"Nope."

Mana giggled. "I'm taking a bath," she said before leaving my room.

There was one week left before the field trip.

I had already forgotten all about it, but Torigoe and Fushimi were awaiting the day with bated breath.

The guidebook for our trip had a section for us to fill out our plans during the group free time. Everyone took notes on it, so I did the same, writing down the schedule we had turned in the other day. Perhaps I wouldn't need it—the Perfect Princess would tell me right away what the next thing on our schedule was if I asked—but just in case.

We didn't have a proper field trip during the third year of middle school; we only had a short day trip elsewhere. Nothing had changed this year, which was why Mana was so jealous when she read the plans for our trip.

"There's gonna be people messing around with each other at night!"

"Why do you think that?"

"It's the field trip we're talking about, y'know?" Mana answered.

Is that really an explanation?

I grabbed the guidebook back and returned to my room, when my phone rang.

It was Torigoe. How unusual.

"What's up?"

"Um... Takamori, good evening."

"Uh, yeah, good evening."

Didn't take her for the type to give proper greetings over the phone.

"Sorry for the sudden call."

"It's no problem."

She stayed silent for a while.

I could hear her try to start talking, then stopping. Was she nervous?

Oh, I get you. Phone calls stress me out, too. I wonder why. I get nervous when I call Shinohara, too.

But if she was going to be this anxious, then why call me?

"Deguchi's a cool guy, huh?" I couldn't take the silence anymore. "Thank you for telling me his name back then."

"No, it was nothing. I could tell you wanted to talk to him, and I knew you didn't know most of our classmates' names."

"Yeah," I replied.

She went silent again.

"On..."

On?

"On our..."

??

"On our second day...during free time...shopping."

"Yeah?" I replied to her faltering speech.

"Free time. It's usually for shopping, y'know, souvenirs and stuff, so um... Would you like to...go shopping.........together?"

She finished speaking after a looong pause. Her voice was so low I was only able to hear her then because it was through the phone.

We were supposed to move as a group during that time anyway, so of course we'd be together.

"Sure. Although, I only have Mana and my mom to buy souvenirs for." I chuckled, and she did, too.

"Just buy something for whoever you want. Could be a classmate."

I guess that's true.

I recalled seeing girls buying souvenirs for each other the year before. I thought it was weird buying souvenirs of the same place you're all visiting, but it must feel good to receive presents.

In any case, I definitely had to buy something for Mana, or else she would retaliate with bad lunches.

"Souvenirs. There we go."

"What?"

"I just noted it down in my guidebook."

"Oh, I'll do the same." She giggled.

After that, we talked some more, and the awkwardness from before completely dissipated.

Once I noticed a whole hour had passed, I said good-bye.

Mana entered my room the instant I hung up.

"Bubby, who were you talking with?"

Again?

"Torigoe. We were making some plans for the field trip."

"You mean the girl as quiet as the forest? *That* Shizu?" Mana looked excited. "W-wait, Bubby. Have you made plans with anyone else?"

"Not on an individual level."

"Oooh! She's the first!"

What are you getting so worked up about?

"Look. I even made a note to buy a souvenir for you."

"Whoa! No cap! I love you, Bubbyyy!"

"Yeah, yeah," I replied to my greedy sister.

No cap was her phrase of the month, by the way.

"I'm betting you will still forget about it either way, though."

That was something that happened often. I couldn't say anything back.

Mana smiled as she sat down on my bed and crossed her legs. Her legs were thin and pale, unlike mine; she took after our mother.

"By the way, a little birdie told me something."

"Hmm?"

"Do you know what Ai was doing in Tokyo?"

"Studying in high school?"

"Yeah, I figured you wouldn't know."

Well, excuse me.

"She was a student, of course, but there's this other thing…"

Then I got a text. I didn't recognize the icon, but the username was Ai.

I think you're the only one without my contact info, it said.

Yup, that's Himeji. I guess Fushimi or Torigoe gave her my handle.

I sent her a sticker with a cartoon dog saying Hi. Took me a while to find it since I didn't use it often.

Good night.

Blunt response. Very Himeji.

"Ai was an idol."

"Huh? No cap?"

"No cap. Hee-hee, now you're using it, too." Mana giggled.

Wonder where the phrase comes from.

"Who knows Ai's an idol? I do," she sang.

Why do you look smug about it?

"Though, it's just a rumor, so it might be cap after all. I asked Ai's brother, Yuuki, but he insists he knows nothing about it. Someone I know who's a fan says she is, but maybe she just looks like that idol." Mana tapped at her phone as she spoke. "It's this group, apparently."

She showed me her search results and pointed at the picture in question.

I could see the resemblance for sure. But who knows?

Mana was showing me an article that said one of the members went on hiatus due to health issues—and then afterward withdrew. This happened a month prior. The story wasn't that uncommon, though it did line up with the timing of her return. The group wasn't a national sensation but was known among the hard-core fans.

"Was she, really…?"

"Maybe Ai got tired of the idol life and came back here because she missed you."

"Why me?"

"…" She sighed hard, like letting out a negative spirit bomb. "I don't think it'd be that weird. She wanted to get away from the big city, leave that past behind, and go back to her beloved childhood friend."

"You're just making stuff up."

"But it could be true!" She stretched her leg out to kick me.

Stop it; I can almost see your panties.

"Geez, you're so dumb."

Why do you feel the need to call me that?

Mana stood up and left my room, but then she came back right away. She looked at my bag and put something inside it.

"What did you just do?"

"You're gonna need it on the field trip."

She looked so sure of it. The trip was still a few days away, though.

"What? Like, earphones or something?"

"Oh, nice guess! Yes, something like that. A small thing that goes a long way in preventing trouble for others."

She left the room again, leaving only that hint behind.

"What is she thinking?"

I had to take a look inside. Love gloves. Three of them, at that.

"Why so many?!"

Not that I'd use even one of them!

It was our daily duty as class reps to write the class journal every day after school and take it to Waka. Only one of us had to do it, but we always waited for the other to finish. Not that day, however.

"Ah… Um, uh, I'll see you, then."

A few of our classmates asked Fushimi to join them at a restaurant to talk about the field trip. The one near the station was their usual hangout. And Fushimi accepted.

"Bye, Ryou," she said, looking down.

Fushimi was an innate people pleaser, so this happened often.

I kind of respected that, actually. Being everybody's friend wasn't an easy thing to do.

"It's fine. I'll go home by myself."

"Yeah…"

She looked like a bunny with ears drooping down.

I was of the opinion she should just turn them down if she didn't want to go, but I suppose she had her own ways of socializing.

As for my other childhood friend, it seemed the transfer student fever had died down already; she was no longer getting mobbed by our class-mates. Although, some guys still came up to her from time to time.

"Hina mentioned it before, but I still can't believe you're so diligent," Himeji said once the classroom became quieter.

"You going home?" I glanced at her, then back at the journal.

"Yeah, in a minute." She had her bag on the desk, ready to go at any moment.

"Okay."

Once we were finally alone, she started talking more. It was about triv-ial stuff—that her uniform would arrive that weekend, so she'd no longer stand out from next week, and other stuff.

I hummed back, cycling through some short responses—oh, cool, huh, wow—as I finished up the journal.

"Aren't you taking too long? Hina does that in, like, five minutes."

"She writes it little by little at the end of every class; that's why."

"You should do that, too."

"Nah, too much trouble."

"And yet you do write it all in the end."

"I mean, I did volunteer for this myself. Gotta do my job."

"You're so weird."

Yeah, it made no sense. If it really was such a pain, I shouldn't have become class rep.

But I didn't have any friends. Having a job to do made me feel like I belonged. That it was okay for me to be a part of this class.

I'd told Fushimi this before, but she only frowned and said she didn't get it.

"It just feels better knowing I'm somebody. That could mean being A's friend, or B's boyfriend, or a member of group C. I have a proper place in the classroom. And I can breathe easier that way."

As it turned out, being "somebody" meant being a class representative. No one else wanted to do it, so it was easy to get. A job anyone could do.

I wasn't expecting her to understand even after the lengthy explanation.

"I kinda know how that feels."

...And apparently I was wrong. "No way."

"Yes way; why would I lie?"

I couldn't believe a pretty girl like her could understand. Fushimi had acted like I'd posed the most complex philosophical question when I told her.

"Anyway...aren't you going home, Himeji?"

"For crying out loud... You still don't get it?" She sighed, staring at me.

I finally finished writing the journal. Not as perfect a record as Fushimi's a day before, but hey. It wasn't because I was lazy—it was Fushimi who took things too seriously. Her notes were always so detailed. Anyone would have trouble following her standards.

I closed the notebook, grabbed my bag, and stood up.

"Is your job done once you give that to Miss Wakatabe?"

"Yeah."

Himeji grabbed her bag, too, and followed behind me.

Although her presence had become commonplace in class, students from different years still did a double take when we came across them in the hallways.

I arrived at the teachers' lounge and handed Waka the journal.

"Thank you," she said before taking a sip of her coffee. She then went back to working on her laptop.

I met back with Himeji at the entrance and changed shoes before leaving.

"Himeji, do you wanna be class rep?"

"No, I was just watching for fun."

"What's fun about that?"

"A lot of things."

Okay…?

The question still gnawing at me, we approached the gates and saw two first-year girls waiting beside it. They glanced at us, then promptly hid in the shadows.

"You're popular, huh, Ryou?"

"Huh?! Me?!"

Am…I? Were they waiting for me?!

My heart was pounding hard as we drew nearer.

"Excuse me!" one of them said.

M-my popular phase is here!

"Hm? What is it?" I replied, my voice cracking.

The girls were not looking at me at all.

"You're Aika, right? From SakuMome."

I immediately knew what was up. Sakurairo Moment was the idol group Mana had told me about, and Aika was the member in question who had left.

"They tell me that a lot, but no, I'm sorry." Himeji smiled at them, then walked away.

"Hey, are you really an idol?" I asked after catching up to her.

"What do you mean *really*?"

"Mana told me there's this rumor about you."

"It's just a rumor."

Should've guessed.

"Would you have liked it if I were? Would it make you glad to think little ol' Ai was a small-time idol?"

"Not really. I would be, like, 'Oh, wow,' but nothing else."

No matter how much she changed, how popular she became, or how evil she turned out, it wouldn't change the fact that she was my childhood friend. And I was hers, too.

"I think I know now why Hina is so head over heels for you."

"What?"

Himeji moved back to the main topic. "It's true. I lied back there."

"...Huh."

Himeji grinned. "There we go. Indifferent, nonchalant, practically apathetic." She cheerfully listed several negative traits.

"...Sorry, okay? That's just how I am."

"But that's exactly why I can tell you. Now, are you gonna post about it on the Internet? Get clout by saying your childhood friend turned out to be an idol?"

"No."

"I know; you're not the type."

Himeji took a few steps ahead, then turned around. "How does it feel to know you kissed an idol?"

"What?"

"At the gym storage room. Before I transferred schools."

So you mean when we were in grade school? Is that why you were asking me if I remembered anything then?

"Well, it wasn't a kiss so much as a peck."

Sure...?

"It was just a moment of love-induced indiscretion."

Wonder if the same thing happened to Fushimi.

"But it was before you became an idol, right?"

"No need to focus on that," she grumbled, then cleared her throat in an exaggerated manner. "Even so, good for you to have a memory you can cherish for the rest of your life, right?"

"Could you be any haughtier?"

"I'm pretty sure that kiss in the storage room with your future-idol childhood friend will flash before your eyes before you die."

"I guess I have no way to deny that as a living person."

"Right?" She laughed. "I'm pretty sure a kiss from me could go for at least a million."

"Don't sell them."

"You don't know a thing about the idol industry, huh?"

"Don't say that."

Himeji beamed in response. "I wasn't sure whether I should tell you; I mean, I really wasn't that big of an idol, and it'd only make me feel bad if you started treating me like some exotic animal. I'm glad that wasn't the case."

It sounded like she'd been having a hard time with that decision.

The group wasn't famous enough to appear on TV and stuff, but it was supposedly well-known among those in the know.

"Good thing I'm so indifferent, huh?"

"I wouldn't tell you if you weren't."

I guess.

"Let's go home," she said as I caught up to her.

"How does it look? Cute?"

Himeji smiled with full confidence as she spun around once.

Just like she'd said, she was finally wearing our school's uniform. It felt weird, like she was cosplaying, even though she was literally in my class.

"Yeah, it looks nice."

"Thank you."

Fushimi then cleared her throat, stood up with a thud, and spun around.

I stared at her, baffled. Himeji chuckled.

After that, Waka entered the classroom wearing her usual rough-and-simple style and took attendance before taking us outside.

"Gosh… I was so excited I couldn't sleep well."

"You're such a kid, Hina."

"Ai… You've got bags under your eyes."

"I'm not falling for that." She snorted.

She did, in fact, have bags under her eyes.

You didn't get any sleep, either, huh?

It was the first day of our field trip. We were about to board buses sorted by class; it would take us two hours to reach our destination.

"D-Deguchi… Mind if we sit together?"

"Sure, that's cool, but…" He paused and looked around.

B-but…what?

"Wouldn't it be more fun if we sat with a girl?" He grinned, as if he had just come up with the best idea of all time.

You think?

I had girls sit beside me on the train pretty frequently, but I wasn't sure that would be comfortable for such a long stretch of time.

"It is the field trip we're talking about. I agree!" Fushimi gave us a thumbs-up.

"Yup. I think this is a good opportunity...," Torigoe agreed in a quiet voice.

I had thought for sure Fushimi and Torigoe would sit together, but I guess not.

"I have no objections. You can sit with me if you want," Himeji added.

Why are you speaking in that tone?

"I bought some snacks. I could give you some if we sit together..." She sneakily showed me a box of Ponky. I'd loved those stick-shaped snacks since I was a kid.

We played rock-paper-scissors to decide the pairs. I used rock, and Deguchi used scissors. The girls also did the same among themselves.

"Rock," I said, raising my hand.

"ROCK!" Fushimi replied with lit-up eyes.

"Torigoe and I both used scissors," Deguchi said.

Himeji was the odd one out.

"Why?!" She pouted.

Yeah, getting left out didn't feel good. And they weren't allowing us to use the auxiliary seats on the bus.

"Sorry, Ai. That's how it goes sometimes." Fushimi gave her a glance of pity.

Himeji's eye twitched. "Don't rub it in."

"There'll be a rest stop, so how about we change it up then?" Torigoe suggested.

"Sounds good," Deguchi agreed.

©Fly

"Yes, I believe that would be an excellent idea." Himeji looked extremely pleased.

Why is she being so formal?

On the other hand, Fushimi's face was devoid of expression.

Anyhow, we decided to change seats at the rest stop.

The teacher in charge of our year gave us a lengthy speech, and then we started boarding the bus.

I got on with my bag and looked around as the seats started filling up, when I saw Fushimi waving at me. I took the aisle seat beside her. Torigoe and Deguchi took the seats in front of us.

"Torigoe brought a book!"

"Ah, um, I…"

"What's it about?"

"Uh, it's…"

She's so nervous.

It was one of those where the Bs fell in L. I only knew because I was aware of what she had been recently reading. I tried to contain my laughter.

"Wonder how Himeji's doing."

"There you go worrying about her again." Fushimi puffed her cheeks.

"I mean, it's just I think it's sad when someone's left out."

Then Himeji folded open the auxiliary seat beside me with a thud and sat down.

"Uh, Himeji, that's…"

The driver spoke through the speakers before I could finish:

"Auxiliary seats are dangerous. Please refrain from using them."

"—!" Himeji was shaking, her face red. I wasn't sure if that was out of embarrassment, but she was trembling badly.

The seat also got in the way for people trying to walk down the aisle.

"Ai, it's okay…"

"You should go grab an empty seat."

"I won't be giving you any Ponky!"

She hugged the snack to her chest as she left to sit a couple rows behind us.

I never said I wanted any in the first place.

Fushimi rifled through her bag and took something out.

"Here. I also brought some, so don't worry."

It was a box of Ponky, the same type as Himeji's.

Why does everyone think I want it?

"You always brought these on field trips."

"I did?"

"I guess Ai also remembers that."

I turned to look behind at her; she was already chatting with another girl. Maybe this outcome was a good thing for her.

And for me, of course.

"Deguchi, I started playing that game you were talking about."

"Oh, really? Want me to add you as a friend?"

"Ah, but I don't have any good supports yet."

"Don't worry about that. Just use mine. I've raised them like my own children."

He gave me his ID, and I sent him a friend request. We talked excitedly about the game while Fushimi and Torigoe chatted about something else.

"Shii, want a Ponky?"

"Thanks. I brought some snacks myself. I'll trade you some later."

"Nice! Snack swapping is a field trip tradition!" Fushimi sounded so glad.

The bus departed, and after a while of noisy chatter, it slowly became quieter. Some people were still chatting, but the voices were low and far away. The two before us were already asleep.

"Ryou, here's your long-awaited Ponky," Fushimi whispered as she opened the box.

"I have not been waiting for this."

She took one stick out and pointed it at me. "Say 'Ah.'"

"No, thank you."

"Hurry. Before someone sees us."

The guys in the seats beside us, and the ones before and behind them, were asleep, too. But who knew when they might wake up.

"The only thing to feel embarrassed about is embarrassment itself."

I don't think that's how it works.

She kept on pointing it at me, so I gave up and took a bite.

"Is it good?"

"Ponky's always good."

"Nice." She beamed. "Now, if you'll excuse me…" She scooched up to me.

"What now?"

"Let's take a pic."

Fushimi opened her camera app and reached out her hand to place the phone in position.

"Huh? Now?"

"Yes, now. And this is only the beginning, okay?"

She switched to the front camera and started snapping away without asking.

"Hey. Stop."

"Hee-hee. Now do a pose."

Snap, snap.

"I don't like having my picture taken."

"Hee-hee. Sorry. But bear with it."

Fushimi finally let me go and swiped through the pictures with a huge grin.

"It's been a while since we took pictures together. It's kinda exciting. Makes your heart skip a beat."

That I agreed with.

"This one stays. This one, too," she happily muttered.

After a lunch stop, we got back on the bus.

Himeji was sitting with me now.

"I'm gonna head over to the others," Fushimi said as she changed seats with Himeji.

Himeji's eyes followed her as she headed for the back of the bus.

"She's acting so cool and composed, like she seems so sure of her standing."

"What do you mean?"

"Nothing, forget about that."

Himeji then took out the box of Ponky from a bag so small one had to wonder if it could fit anything else.

"You don't want some?"

I never said I did.

I mean, I like them, but Fushimi already gave me some...

"Not right now."

"Please. No need to feel embarrassed about it."

How did we reach this conclusion?

She kept holding the box toward me until finally she grabbed a couple and started eating them herself.

Looks like you wanted them all along.

"Hey, Takayan, wanna play cards?" Deguchi said, poking his head out the side of his seat.

Takayan? Is that me? Huh... Not bad. Nice nickname.

"Takamori sounds too cool for you, so." He cackled.

"It does?" I tilted my head.

Torigoe also peeked at us and said, "I brought cards."

"You came prepared, huh."

"Gimme a sec," she said as she looked for them in her bag.

Meanwhile, Himeji had her cheeks stuffed with Ponky; she hurriedly chewed like a hamster and swallowed.

"I'll play, too."

You were pretty desperate to say that, huh? There's still Ponky crumbles on your mouth.

We started playing old maid with Torigoe's cards. It was surprisingly fun.

"Hey, Himeji, I can see your whole hand from that angle."

"I'm showing it to you. I know you wouldn't take advantage of it."

"Stop using my goodwill against me."

"Takayan, you got the joker, don't you?"

"…No."

""""He does!""""

How could you tell?

We played a few times, and I lost over half the games.

"Takamori, you're an open book."

"Really?"

"Takayan… How do you hide your dirty thoughts?"

"I am most definitely not having dirty thoughts right now, so don't worry."

"So that means you do have them sometimes, huh."

"Himeji, stop trying to trip me up."

"We should've bet on something, man," Deguchi said, sounding disappointed.

"Since Takamori sucks at this, let's do something else." Torigoe looked through her bag and took out a different deck of cards.

"Another card game?" I asked.

"No, tarot."

"You can do that, Torigoe?" Deguchi asked.

"A bit. I looked into it some time ago."

"..." Himeji stared attentively in silence.

"Himeji, do you like fortune-telling?" Torigoe asked.

"Not really. I always forget whatever they say after three days or so."

"You heard her, Torigoe. Don't tell her fortune," I said.

"However. I am willing to let Shizuka do it so she can practice her skills."

Just be honest.

"Himejima, just say you like it," Deguchi said with a small smile.

"I always say exactly what I think," she replied.

Fortune-telling started with Deguchi. He followed Torigoe's instructions, visualizing what she told him to and picking the cards. After she revealed her interpretation, he exclaimed in wonder.

"I feel like that's right... Are you serious?"

"You might have that sort of meeting in the near future, according to the card you chose and its position."

"Thank you so much, wise master."

"You're welcome."

Okay...

Himeji cleared her throat then.

"Okay, okay. It's your turn, Himeji."

"...Thank you."

Himeji settled down after seeing Deguchi's reaction.

She followed the same steps in that five-minute process.

"Mm-hmm. You have it rough, Himeji."

"Huh?"

"That's what the cards tell me. But things should take a turn for the better due to changes in your environment."

"…Thank you so much, wise master. I will do my best in order to achieve that."

"You are welcome."

Seriously, what's up with all this?

"Looks like I'm next. Let's do this." I did the same thing as them.

"Hmm. I see."

"What?"

"There's been a change lately, hasn't there?"

Himeji's return? That's all I can think of.

"A small breakthrough for you. Something that will trigger change in your life."

"Will it?"

"You may fall in love with someone close to you. Or not."

Make up your mind.

"The cards say that you might be better off with the dandelion on the side of the road, rather than the sunflower at its peak or the dazzling rose…" Her voice started trailing off.

"Torigoe, you're getting red in the face."

Then she hid behind her seat. Himeji followed by poking her head through the side.

"Shizuka, is that really what the cards say, or is it just what you want them to say?"

"It's what they said."

"Why so red, then?" She poked Torigoe's cheek.

"I'm always red."

"You're so naive."

"…"

Deguchi looked at them with clear, pure eyes. "Lilies…"

"Lilies…?"

"We men must never set foot in that realm, Takayan. Remember that."

Only thing I got was that I definitely didn't need to remember any of what he said.

Himeji leaned back in her seat and sighed. "Geez, can't even let your guard down for a second."

"Maybe Torigoe only looks naive to you because you have lots of experience in the adult world," I said nonchalantly.

She giggled. "If you really think that, then I'm sure you'll like me more and more as you continue to get to know me."

...Where's that confidence coming from?

"No, I won't."

"Ha-ha. You're such a kid."

Shut it.

"Oh, don't get sulky about it."

"I am not."

Deguchi was still looking at us, but then he heaved a heavy sigh and turned around.

"Wise master, I just experienced great pain," he said.

"What is it, my student?" Torigoe replied.

"I saw a couple of teens flirting behind us."

"Oh dear, how vile."

You're still keeping that act up?

The inn we arrived at was a simple one—and very tidy. Deguchi and I ended up in a room with three guys from another group. All other rooms were similar: five or six people per room, separated by gender.

It was a typical Japanese inn. The room was equipped with a teapot and teacups, and one of the guys started making tea as soon as we got there.

"Hey, uh, we're supposed to only leave our stuff here and get going right away," I told him.

"Really?" he replied, then looked at his guidebook.

To be fair, I wouldn't be as aware of the schedule if I wasn't class rep. So I didn't blame the guy for not knowing.

"Degucchi, you're in that group with Himejima, Fushimi, and SB Torigoe, right? I'm so jealous."

"Right? The late bird gets the worm, you see," Deguchi said proudly.

The other guys seemed to be his friends, and they started talking about their own groups.

"Oh man, that sounds so fun," he said, clearly enjoying the conversation.

Yeah... Of course he's not just my friend, he's everyone's friend.

"I heard some rumors that Himejima's an idol... Is that true?"

Deguchi turned toward me, shocked.

I feigned ignorance. She didn't tell her secret to anyone, so it wasn't my place to talk about it.

"Imagine that... Going to her concert, seeing her sing and dance, and then getting the chance to see her smile and shake her hand. I'd totally fall in love."

"I get you, brother."

"Anyway, it's almost time to gather in the lobby. Let's go," I said.

They all replied half-heartedly, grabbed only the necessities, and left the room.

I walked behind the relatively noisy group of three, while Deguchi followed by my side.

"So...is it true?" he asked, voice low.

"What?"

"That thing about Himejima."

"I dunno. First time I heard about it."

That was the most I could say. Rumors were quick to spread. I mean, even stuff like couples dating in secret became public knowledge within seconds.

"...I see."

"And if it's true, wouldn't it mean she's no longer an idol now? She won't sing and dance. Or smile at randos and shake their hand."

She only does that for money, apparently.

"Still, isn't it nice to think about? What a dream, to have an idol transfer to your school."

"Who dreams about that?"

"Are you serious? All high schoolers."

"Well, I don't."

"Whatever you say."

Once everyone was gathered in the lobby, we headed toward the buses.

I wonder what room Fushimi and the girls ended up in.

I grabbed my guidebook, already so wrinkly on the first day of our trip, and saw they were in a room with three others from a different group.

We had a map of the inn showing everyone's rooms, in case of emergencies, but every time, I worried about some idiot using the information for evil.

"Everyone's here! Let's go!"

We followed Waka's order and got on our bus again. This time, I sat beside Torigoe.

"Takamori, where are we going next?"

"Um, uh…to a shrine for this famous military commander."

"And what domain was he famous for leading?"

"A pop quiz?!"

"I know!" Fushimi, sitting in front of us, raised her hand. Beside her was Himeji.

"Nobody asked you, Hiina."

"Do you know, Ryou?"

"…I do, but I don't wanna say it." I glanced out the window.

Himeji cackled, "Ha-ha-ha. You don't know, do you?"

"I'll just learn it later, okay? What's the big deal?" I confessed.

Fushimi and Torigoe laughed, too.

After thirty or so minutes, we arrived at the shrine. There were very few visitors, perhaps because it was a weekday—perfect for looking around at our leisure.

"We have to write a report about this later, remember? You should take some notes," Fushimi told me specifically.

Why did you single me out? Tell the others, too.

"I know, I know."

"I don't see a pen in your hand!"

"I have my phone."

"Kids these days!"

Okay, Grandma.

She really did bring a notebook and pen.

"Hiina, they're allowing us to use our phones to take pictures and all, so why bring a notebook?"

Torigoe, too, was a total zoomer. She was taking pictures of everything while taking notes on her phone.

"I can remember things better this way," Fushimi replied.

In my own experience, there hadn't been a single time where taking notes helped me. Often, I had a hard time even deciphering my own writing when I tried to review them.

Besides, information from books or the Internet was better organized than anything I could put together. And not once had I ever actually written an extensive report for this sort of thing.

"Hina, Ryou said he wants to take a picture with me. Mind taking it for us?"

"I never said that."

Himeji completely ignored my comment and looked around for the best place to use as the background, then dragged me over there.

"Ai, Ryou never said that. Are you hallucinating? Are you feeling okay? Should I go call the nurse?" Fushimi looked seriously worried about her.

The school nurse had come on the field trip, too, but wasn't near us at the moment.

"I-I'm fine! He was acting like he wanted to, okay?"

"No, I wasn't."

"Ai?" Fushimi prompted.

Himeji took the phone from my hands and handed it over to Fushimi. "I know what you two did on the bus," Himeji said.

"…!" Fushimi's face stiffened. "O-okay, okay…but you just get one." She held the phone in position with a stiff smile.

What about my wishes?

"Hiina, what are you doing?" Torigoe came, too. "Ah, I see, I see. Very well."

"You're still not letting Himejima go! Takayan, you traitor!" Deguchi whined.

"Huh? Ryou, what did you do with Ai?" Fushimi put down the phone, smiling, but her eyes were very serious.

""They were flirting,"" Deguchi and Torigoe said in unison.

"Really?"

Fushimi tightened her grip on my phone, looking as if she might crush it. Uncanny dark flames seemed to wave behind her.

"Fushimi, please, calm down. Breathe in... Breathe out. We were not flirting."

And give me back my phone. I don't care about photos.

"How about we find a happy medium where I take a picture with Takamori instead?"

How is that a happy medium, Torigoe?

Torigoe slowly inched over to my side while my two childhood friends battled through their glares and had Deguchi help her take a few pictures of us.

"I-I'll send them to you later."

"S-sure."

"...Looks like I should make my move, too..."

No. Don't move an inch, Deguchi. And what's with that look on your face?

In the end, I took a picture with everyone. Including Deguchi.

"Why you, too?"

"Oh, I'm just going with the flow. Would be weird not to, don't you think?"

How?

Fushimi gave us a heartwarming look when she took my photo with Deguchi.

Then we had someone from another group take a picture of all of us together.

I got it afterward through a text, and we all looked so happy. It was a good photo.

After walking around the shrine's premises, we walked down the samurai residence street nearby, went to a famous temple, and that was it for our outside activities for the first day.

On the bus back to the inn, Deguchi asked, "Takayan, what's the difference between a shrine and a temple?"

"Don't ask me."

"Huh? I thought you were smart."

"No, that's Fushimi. Don't think that I'm smart just because I'm class rep."

"Gotcha."

He was sitting beside me. In front of us were Torigoe and Fushimi. Himeji was alone at the back.

Photos got uploaded one by one to the group chat we made for that purpose. They were all from Fushimi and Torigoe.

"This one's nice."

"Yeah, look at these faces."

They were carefully selecting photos from among the many they took. Some of them had all five of us, some of them only two, and some of them three.

"Photos of Fushimi, Himejima, and Torigoe... I could sell these," Deguchi muttered.

On my phone, I had more videos than photos. Most of them were only ten seconds long—people having fun, looking silently at the gardens, that sort of stuff.

"Oh, nice."

"Hey, don't look!"

I turned off my screen as soon as I noticed he was peeking.

"I like that one of Fushimi gazing wistfully into the distance, where she notices she's being filmed and gets nervous, then bashfully makes a pose. That one's good, director."

"Stop it."

Hearing it like that only made it more embarrassing.

I wasn't actually practicing for the movie—I just saw people taking photos and videos, so I tried it out myself.

"That would sell like hotcakes."

"We are not selling this."

He must really want to make this a business, huh? He asked me to send it to him, but I strongly refused.

When I took this video of Fushimi, Himeji had noticed and said, "Film me, too, if you want." I did not want to, at all. But I obliged, since it clearly mattered to her.

She was definitely photogenic, but she was too aware of that; her attempts to act cool for the camera didn't feel natural.

The storage on my phone was already filling up with videos.

Once we arrived back at the inn, Waka explained what we would do next. She only repeated what was written in the guidebook, but considering how many people don't pay attention or read the guide properly—like me—this sort of announcement was appreciated.

We had some free time before dinner at the inn. Dinner was Japanese-style, mainly seafood and tempura. After that, we went back to our rooms.

The only thing remaining was to wait for bath time, then sleep.

"Why do the girls get thirty minutes per class, while we only get fifteen, Prez?!"

"Don't ask me."

The roommate was half kidding about his complaint. But I did remember the same thing happening the year prior. I had to get out in a hurry.

"Wait. Boys and girls go in at different times?" another boy in my room asked.

"Obviously."

You think they'd let us go in together?

"Prez, do something about it!"

"I can't."

You really think I could?

"Don't you want to hear the girls chatter and giggle in the bath next door?"

Everyone else, save for me, strongly agreed.

"You'd only need one of the girls to report it, and it's over. Forget about it."

Why did someone have to suggest this every single time?

"No, no, Prez. We're only sitting in the bath. That's all. The sound would come over from the other side; nothing we can do about it."

I'm sure what you intend on doing is listening carefully, and that's different from just hearing.

"Peeping is a thing of the past. It's the era of sound-only."

What?

The other three were giving him high fives.

"…I don't think that's right, either."

Just as their spirits were sky-high about the evolution of bath spying, someone knocked at the door.

"Come in."

It was Fushimi, wearing a *yukata*. She had her hair tied up, something I rarely saw.

"Excuse me…" She poked her head in.

Everyone, except me, lowered their hips and slouched, frozen in time.

"What's up?"

"Hey, Ryou, do you have a phone charger?"

"Oh, sure."

Before I could grab my bag, all four guys were kneeling before her, offering their own charger.

"Please, take mine..."

"No, his stinks. And mine charges quicker."

"Princess, mine charges five times faster than his."

"Please, take good care of it, Fushimi, and hopefully you remember me when you use it."

Fushimi's eyes widened, then she laughed out loud.

"Thanks, but I'm not comfortable borrowing other people's chargers. I'll just take Ryou's."

"Torigoe didn't bring hers? Or anyone else?"

"Oh... They're all charging their own phones. I figured yours still has some battery left, so."

How do you know how much battery I've got left?

Well, I wasn't using my phone all the time, so she probably guessed.

"Okay. Here." I threw the charger at her, and she caught it. "Well done."

"Hee-hee. Thanks," she said before leaving.

"She only has eyes for Takayan..."

"Must be good, being so close to her..."

"Am I just a side character in some manga? This guy's definitely the protagonist."

"I don't even need a girlfriend! Just something similar... I just wanna be close to a girl like that."

Their spirits had taken a nosedive.

Guys... She just didn't take yours because your chargers don't work with her phone.

"This sucks."

They were still grumbling while grabbing their stuff for bathing.

""""Where's *my* childhood friend?"""""

I had to open a window to let out all the CO_2 they exhaled.

After a while, my phone vibrated with a text from Fushimi.

I forgot to ask!

what? I typed in reply.

Then a picture popped up. It was a selfie of her in a *yukata*.

Does it look nice on me?

After a closer look, I saw that her chest was slightly exposed. Maybe because she took it in a hurry? Anyway, I instinctively looked away.

"Is she…?"

I don't think she's doing it on purpose.

I cleared my throat and started typing a reply, my eyes squinting at the screen, when I got a new message. The photo above was already gone.

Why did it turn out suggestive?!?!

don't ask me

My theory was that her chest was so flat that a gap was created.

you could just wear a tracksuit y'know? no need for a yukata

Where's the charm in that?

And why do you need that?

Anyway! You saw nothing! I'll send you a new one!

it looked fine, don't worry

I don't believe you!

She sent a sticker of an angry cartoon character.

go take that bath already

Girls are going later

I looked around and noticed I was alone.

Right. Boys and girls are going at different times.

Wonder who they'll be listening intently to.

It's time for you to take a bath, Ryou.

everyone already went but ill do it later

Naughty!

©Fly

The inn's website said their baths were open until eleven PM. I didn't have to take that hurried fifteen-minute bath now, did I? I guessed the schedule was set in order to not bother other guests.

I decided to watch some TV in the meanwhile, when someone knocked at the door.

Did one of the guys forget something?

That wasn't the case.

"I told you. I'm not a good girl…" Fushimi locked the door behind her.

She took off her slippers and approached me, taking care not to step on the futons. Mine was all the way in the corner, near the window.

She sat down on it, and the tension in the air was rising.

"…Don't lock the door."

"Oh, I already did. Because I'm a bad girl." She giggled. "What're you watching?" She glanced at the TV.

It was a variety show, nothing special. It wasn't like I followed it every week, but I couldn't concentrate on it with Fushimi by my side.

Once the commercial break started, she poked at my knee.

"What?"

"You took pictures with Ai and Shii."

"Yeah."

"You looked so giddy about it."

"I did not."

"You totally did!" She sulked. Even though none of that actually happened. "You should only take pictures with your childhood friend!"

"Who came up with that rule?"

"What if they frame the photos?!"

No one's going to do that.

Fushimi's cheeks turned red, like she had just gotten out of the bath. She huffed and then pushed me down aggressively.

"Ow! What's wrong with you?"

"You're on the futon; you'll be fine."

I tried to raise myself back up, but then she leaned over and tried to hold me, and I fell back down.

"Fushimi?"

"Ryou... You're too kind to everyone. I don't like that."

She put her face on my chest and looked up at me.

"Fushimi, your *yukata*...is slipping off a bit."

"It's fine as long as it's just a bit."

It's not. I can already see about 20 percent of your distinctly modest chest.

"Wiggle, wiggle." She went under the blanket and then covered me with it, too.

"Thank— Wait, no. What the hell are you doing?"

"Ah-ha-ha-ha-ha. This is so fun," she said as she wiped her tears with her index finger.

She was totally red. I totally would have assumed she just got out of the bath if the girls hadn't had their turn yet.

"Fushimi, were you drinking?"

"...No."

"What did you drink?"

"It looked like juice."

So it wasn't juice!

"When did you drink that?!" *And who gave it to you? Someone in your room?* "Geez. You really are bad."

"I'm just like you. Hee-hee." She rolled around, trying to get me to hug her.

"We can't let the guys see us like this."

"That's why I locked the door."

No! Bad!

I could hear noise from outside.

"Ryou."

"Hmm? ...Wait, I hear something outside."

"It's fine. No one will notice so long as I stay inside your futon!"

Hmm, I guess that's true... Wait, no! This ain't no 4D pocket!

What's going on outside, though, really? While my attention was focused on the door, Fushimi slowly inched her body closer to mine.

"Ryou."

"What?"

"Won't you…kiss me?"

I nearly choked on my own saliva.

"N-no, I won't… There are rules about these things…"

"But we've already kissed, remember? You're so uptight in the weirdest ways."

She poked my face with her nose.

Clack! The door opened with a metallic chime.

Huh? Wasn't that locked…? And the key…is right there, beside the TV.

"Prez, please don't lock the door like that."

"He never came to the bathroom, huh."

"Where's he now?"

Crap, the master key! They asked for it from the staff. So that's what all the noise was about.

Now it's over. They're gonna think we were doing something *if they find Fushimi…and in my futon, no less.*

"What now, Ryou? They'll catch us."

You sure sound like you're having the time of your life, huh?

I couldn't let them find her drunk like this, either.

I had no choice. I swiftly opened the closet beside us and threw her in there.

"Huh? What was that foooor?"

"Keep quiet."

Then I dived back into my futon and pretended to be asleep.

"Heeey, Prez…?"

"The dude's sleeping."

"Guess that explains why he didn't open the door."

"Takayaaan, it's morning!" Deguchi shook my body.

I had to get everyone out of the room to give Fushimi a chance to escape. There was no other way.

"Ah...sorry; I fell asleep."

"You're sure a heavy sleeper!"

Everyone laughed.

Fushimi slightly slid open the closet door, peering at us.

I got up in a hurry and closed it again behind my back.

"I—I don't like it here; it's all dark..."

"Deal with it."

"Takayan, what's wrong?"

"Uh...nothing." I smiled back.

I let the guys chat for a while, and every time she made a noise behind me, I deliberately coughed or sneezed loudly to distract everyone from it.

"H-how about we go...visit the girls' room?"

"C-can we really do that?"

"Long as the teachers don't notice."

"They must be missing us, too... I'm sure they want to play cards with us."

They're gonna get mad at you, for sure.

"Takayan, let's go. We rise or fall together."

C-crap, now they want me to join, too.

We high-fived...for some reason.

"O-okay, let's go."

With brave expressions, they grabbed only their phones and left. I was trusted with the key.

Once everyone was in the hallway, Fushimi came out of the closet and left the room. I let out a sigh of relief.

We made it... Mission accomplished.

"Good night," she said before walking in the opposite direction from us.

I hurried to catch up with the guys, but by the time I saw them, they were already walking back to the room, complaining about being caught in the teachers' tight security web.

"Let's just play by ourselves," Deguchi said.

"Yes, let's do that, guys," I strongly agreed.

Everyone looked suspicious at my energetic response at first, but then they chuckled.

"Didn't know you liked cards that much, Takayan!"

"Okay then, let's give Prez what he wants."

They all nodded happily, and so began the card tournament in our room.

The card games with the guys were more fun than I expected. We only played old maid, but we didn't get tired of it. The reason was simple.

"Everyone has to say whose panties they'd like to see once they clear their hands."

"Hold on. Shouldn't that sort of punishment be for the loser?"

"Sounds great! Let's do this!"

"You really want to answer that question?"

We started the game under those ridiculous conditions and chatted.

"So who is it, Degucchi?"

"I'll tell you once I'm out."

"Is it a girl? A boy?"

"A girl, right?" I said.

"So you already have someone in mind, huh, Prez?" The guy poked my side with his elbow.

"No, I mean, we are talking about girls here, right?"

"Yeah. No fun in talking about dudes," Deguchi said.

I took a card from the guy beside me, formed a pair to discard, then had the guy on the other side grab one of mine. The rules of the game itself were still the same.

"I'm done." The guy right in front of me discarded his last pair, then looked me in the eye. "Doesn't feel good saying it to your face, but... Fushimi. I'm for real."

"The orthodox answer."

"Yeah, I guess."

"Safe answer."

You wanna see Fushimi's panties? Really?

The game went on, and I had to think of who I'd say when I was done.

"Done!" the guy to my right said, then named a girl from third year, from the same club as him. "Though, well, it's not so much a wish as something that's already happened a few times."

"Seriously?"

"Did it happen during club or something?"

Deguchi also finished just as they were asking the question. "Only one choice for me... Waka."

""""Ohh!"""" Everyone agreed.

I wondered then why guys got so excited over this topic.

Only this other guy and I were left, and then I pulled the joker.

"Being completely serious about this..." He named a girl from the next class over.

"Who?" someone asked. "Oh, that girl," someone else said, bringing her face to mind.

Now, then. Time for the next match...

I started gathering the cards, when I felt everyone's stares on me.

"Takayan... You know what to do now, right?"

"I don't want to know."

"You gotta say a name, too, Prez." He tapped my shoulder.

O-okay. Fine.

"...You know the girl who came for teaching practice? For world history... Hoshino."

The teacher-in-training we had a month or so prior.

"Oh, that's a good choice."

"A college-age girl, huh."

"All of us were kids, looking only at what we had within our reach."

"Takayan... You've got good taste."

I just named someone that wouldn't cause problems. I was shocked to get that much praise.

"Hey, it's lights-out time!" The teacher on patrol came in the room and shouted.

We hurried back to our futons and pretended to be asleep until he left. The room went quiet after the door closed.

There in the darkness, someone chuckled, and it got me to laugh, too.

"Hey, Takayan, so you like older women?"

"Not really... And you have no place calling me out for that; you named Waka."

"Ha-ha. Yeah."

I could tell he was scratching his nose proudly.

Lights were off, but nobody fell asleep. We kept on talking, mostly about romance.

As I listened to them, I was amazed at the fact that boys did this, too.

The conversation began by discussing how to ask girls out, and how to hold a conversation building up to it.

With the way the conversation was flowing, I figured I could talk about *that* without them knowing it had really happened to me.

"What would you do if a girl kissed you out of the blue?"

"It depends on who it was, but I'd be shocked...," one guy said.

"Who is it? Describe the setting."

"Let's say it's a classmate you get along with."

"I think I wouldn't be able to take her off my mind after that."

Ah... Yeah, I know that feeling.

Sure enough, I had been thinking more about her ever since, like I was under the effect of a spell or something.

"Guys, I think he's talking about something that really happened," someone else said.

It did... but I gotta deny it.

"No, I was just asking..."

"""""No way.""""" They spoke in unison.

"How did you even think we wouldn't notice?"

"I'm sure we'd find out that you're all red in the face if we turned on the lights, Takayan."

"Sh-shut up! Yes, it's true!" I confessed.

They roared with laughter.

"So did you fall in love?" asked Deguchi, I think.

"I wouldn't fall in love just because of that… But honestly, I don't know." It felt like the darkness allowed me to open up. "But I'm thinking about it. I'm still thinking about it."

Even though it's been a while since the incident, I was still stuck on it—maybe Shinohara was right about me. Gutless and a pain to deal with.

"This feels serious… So I am seriously thinking about it."

I wasn't sure I was explaining myself right. Couldn't there be a clearer way to say what I was getting at?

"You're so mature, Prez."

"…I would've totally rushed without thinking about it."

There were times where I felt that way, too—that maybe I didn't have to think so much about it.

"Must be a very special person to you if you're thinking about it this carefully, huh, Takayan?"

"I suppose."

"Good. That's nothing weird. Think things through as much as you want."

Really?

"I think that's what sincerity is all about."

Sincerity… Huh.

I'd never thought about it like that.

On the second day of the field trip, I got a text from Mana in the morning.

How's it going? Having fun?

That was all, so it was easy to type a reply.

We had breakfast, changed clothes, and so began the second day.

We had to visit a set of predetermined tourist spots and have the teacher stamp our visits in the guidebook. We could take any route or detour we wanted so long as we completed it within the time frame. It was much more of a typical tourist trip compared to what we did on the first day.

"Let's follow the schedule, okay?" Fushimi said, studying the guidebook, once we gathered at the inn's entrance.

She was adamant about following the schedule.

"The bus is departing in ten minutes, so let's go!"

"It wouldn't really affect us if we took the next one."

"No, no. If you keep thinking like that, we'll be late coming back."

C'mon, the schedule's not that tight.

"What if some delinquents get in our way or something?"

"You're really worrying about that?"

No way that's happening.

"We just have to see everything within the set time frame, right? Why should we follow your uptight schedule, Hina?" Himeji said, surprisingly on the same page as me.

"Hiina's schedule is perfectly drafted to give us enough time for everything, so we can take it easy if we follow it," said Torigoe.

"Right!" Fushimi puffed her chest.

How in the world did this diligent girl end up with alcohol in her system?

Considering she compared it to juice, it probably wasn't beer—more like a cocktail or maybe hard seltzer. But there was no way she bought it herself.

"Last night's card game was so fun, Takayan."

"Yeah, wanna play more tonight?"

"Nah, let's do something different this time around."

"Sure."

Fushimi heard us talking. "You played cards last night?"

"Yeah, did you want to join, too?" Deguchi said.

"Would you have let me join if I asked?"

"Of course. Were you that sad, not getting to play cards with us?"

Who gets sad over not being able to play cards?

"Hiina, you can't go to the boys' room. You'll get in trouble."

"Not if no one notices."

"Can I join, too?" Himeji asked.

We nodded. No reason to turn her down.

"Okay, then what about me?" Torigoe asked.

"Everyone's welcome!"

I had a feeling tonight would be a long one.

Fushimi led the way like a teacher, and once we got to the bus stop, she pulled out her notes and told us where we'd be going and how much the fare would be.

There were other groups there, too. A crowd gathered around Fushimi and Himeji, and they talked as we waited for the bus. Fushimi was popular to begin with, but with Himeji, excitement about a transfer student was still strong with people from other classes. Nothing unusual.

Also expected was that Torigoe, Deguchi, and I were left out of this circle.

"Hey, Torigoe, did something happen in your guys' room last night?" I asked.

"Not really?"

"Fushimi was acting weird yesterday, around the time the boys got in the bath."

"...Really?"

"She said she drank some 'juice.'"

"Is there any problem with drinking juice?"

Torigoe didn't seem to know about it.

Soon enough the bus came, and after twenty minutes or so, we arrived at our first destination: the art museum. They had a contemporary art exhibition going on.

The teacher waiting before the reception desk gave us the tickets and stamped our guidebooks.

Fushimi had planned for two hours there, but we toured the whole thing in just over an hour.

We sat down on the sofas near the lobby to rest awhile.

"That sure was...c-contemporary," Fushimi kindly commented. Her smile was stiffer than usual.

"Yeah. Sure. Nice museum," Deguchi added.

I had no idea what I saw, either. It was the first time I'd taken the time to check out contemporary art, and it all went way over my head.

"What in the world was that? A garbage expo?" Himeji did not mince words; Fushimi's tactful efforts went down the drain.

Himeji only glanced once at each piece during our tour, hurrying us to move on every time.

"But there was a certain pattern to it all, right? Like there were some inspired by artists before them, arranging the pieces with their own unique twist." Torigoe showed the most interest out of all of us. She seemed to have liked it quite a bit.

"Okay. I think the expo wasn't for a more general audience," Himeji said.

I nodded in agreement a couple times.

Then Fushimi started whining that we had to take a picture at the museum and got the teacher to take it for us.

"Man… My gallery's gonna be loaded with treasures," Deguchi said with closed eyes.

"They're just photos, dude."

He clicked his tongue in response, waving his index finger. "You don't get it, Takayan. You see, you can't just ask a girl to take a picture with you. They'll think you're trying to hit on them."

"Do they, really?"

"They do! Especially the more middle-of-the-road ones."

I tilted my head in confusion. I glanced at my childhood friends, who were totally listening to us, and asked, "Fushimi, Himeji, would you think that?"

""Not at all.""

"Takayan, you're talking to the top of the food chain there."

So I tried asking the same thing to Torigoe, probably lower on the "food chain."

"I…would…probably think that. L-like, maybe, yeah, I would wonder, if he kinda likes me…," she muttered.

"Torigoe, let's take a picture!"

"No. Go away. I can see right through you."

"Nooo!!" Deguchi screamed to the heavens.

"Deguchi said 'Especially the middle-of-the-road girls,' but I'll tell you now, Torigoe, you're not middle of the road at all." I knew Deguchi hadn't meant any harm, so I tried to help prevent him from embarrassing himself too much.

"Ah… Thanks… Takamori."

Our break time was over, and we headed to our next destination: a Japanese garden. Fushimi told us all about it on our way there.

"You really are so smart, Fushimi," Deguchi remarked.

"Nah, I just looked it up beforehand."

The two of them were walking at the front, while Torigoe and I followed behind. Even farther behind was Himeji.

"Did something happen in your room last night?" I asked.

"Hmmm… I guess something did happen."

"What?"

"Silly love talk. We chatted over some snacks and drinks."

Pretty normal field trip stuff.

"So you talked about who you like and all that?"

"Some did. Not me."

"Nothing?"

"Nothing."

I couldn't picture her jumping into that sort of conversation, so that was no surprise. But I could imagine her sitting there, listening in silence.

"Did you want me to tell them?"

"Huh? Tell them what?" I didn't understand what she was getting at.

She grinned mischievously.

"That I got turned down, but I still like him." She stared right in my eyes as she said that; I was at a loss for words. "I wouldn't tell them. Or anyone. I'd only tell that to Mii."

She and Shinohara sure were close friends.

After that, Torigoe slowed down her pace, matching Himeji's.

The teacher stamped our guidebook once we arrived at an apparently famous garden, and we strolled around it.

It was already lunchtime, and groups were free to eat wherever they chose, so we ate at the atmospheric soba shop in the garden.

I would've preferred something quicker and more filling, like fast food. I muttered my opinion out loud, and Fushimi was not pleased.

"Ryou, you lack a sense of culture."

"And you don't?"

"No. You see, you eat Japanese cuisine at a very Japanese place. Simple."

Too simple, ain't it?

Deguchi adopted a very enlightened expression as we left the restaurant.

"That was an exceptionally cultured tempura soba," he said.

Acting like you know what you're saying now?

By the way, I ate *kitsune* soba.

"This matcha ice cream is quite cultured, indeed."

"Yes, so very cultured," Himeji said, taking a bite of Torigoe's ice cream.

They just wanted to say the word.

We ended up spending a lot of time in the garden, all because Fushimi and Deguchi wanted to take photos at every turn.

There were two spots we still had to visit after: the castle park near the garden and a market.

The park wasn't that different from the garden (as far as I could tell), so we only got the stamp and walked over to the bus for the market.

All five of us sat down in the rearmost row. We were staring out the windows when Himeji muttered, "It's so nice visiting another town."

"So cultured."

"Indeed."

"Fushimi, do you think matcha sweets are cultured?" Deguchi asked.

"No."

"Reallyyy?"

The word had become a joke between us.

We got off at the bus stop nearest to the market and looked for the teacher—Waka, this time—to stamp our guidebook.

Some unnecessary thoughts crossed my mind as I saw her, all because of Deguchi's silly comments the night prior.

"All according to schedule, huh, class reps? There's still two hours left; don't go crazy, okay? I'm talking to you, Deguchi," said Torigoe.

"Wuh? Me?"

"I doubt Takamori would go crazy. Or any of the girls."

"So I take it your eyes are all on me, wise master?"

"Not in a good way, young pupil."

Seemed like Deguchi had it worse than me.

The fish market was a shopping arcade; the street had so many stalls selling seafood.

"Ryou, look! That looks so good!" Fushimi excitedly grabbed me by the arm and dragged me with her.

They were selling scallops, grilled and buttered. Five hundred yen a plate. Pretty hefty price... But it did look good. Fushimi bought one, and I got tempted to buy one as well. Then everyone did.

"This is pretty good."

We were eating as we walked.

Deguchi glanced over at the entrance to the market and said, "Waka's so great, dude."

"I could agree with you on that, but care to explain how, exactly?"

"She's twenty-nine, English teacher... Ain't that sexy?"

"How, exactly?"

"She's not too cute or pretty; she's just in-between, and that's what makes her great."

"Dude, look at her. She's all alone over there, waiting for more students to come."

"I'll go bring her some scallops!"

And so he went. Bought an extra portion of it and hurried back to the entrance.

"I feel like Deguchi would be fine with any woman," Torigoe said.

I couldn't disagree.

"Aren't all boys like that?" Himeji said, shrugging.

"No, Ai. Ryou's not like that."

"No, he's the same. All men are the same below the surface."

"He's not!"

"You just want to believe that, Hina. But I'm not that idealistic, you know? *I* won't be shocked when I find out the truth."

"Uh-huh. And so what?"

"…" Himeji frowned.

Ugh. It's gonna be a long one. And I'm definitely going to get hit if I try to calm them down.

Once again, I was reminded that there was no one Fushimi could argue with like this other than Himeji.

"Now that they're having fun, let's go," Torigoe said.

"Oh, right."

Yeah, that thing we said we'd do.

"Are they always like that?" she asked.

"Not *always*, but it's pretty common for them to argue like that when there's a trigger."

"I guess they're really close."

"They're just childhood friends." Then I thought I could try asking about that thing again. "Hey, did Fushimi drink anything weird last night?"

"As far as I saw, she only drank juice…but she got bizarrely worked up after our love talk, and she left for a while."

Yeah…that must've been when she came to our room.

So she didn't drink something that "looked like juice." It really was just juice. She may have seemed drunk, but she was probably influenced by whatever they discussed, like Torigoe said.

"So you're buying a souvenir for your sister?"

"Of course."

Don't want her to make me a bad lunch.

"I'll buy something for her, too. Mind giving it to her?"

"Yeah, no problem. She'll be really happy."

"You get along so well with your sister. I'm the oldest of four, so I find that hard to do."

She's the oldest? Huh, I figured she was an only child.

She had two brothers and one sister. Both her parents worked, so she had to take care of the housework.

"...Didn't pin you as the kind."

"I didn't really want to talk about it before, but I figured it's fine."

"Why didn't you want to?"

"Considering my whole personality, I don't really want any pity for having a poor family on top of that."

A quiet girl who did all the housework for her brothers and sister... Huh.

"I dunno what girls would think, but that probably gets you points from guys."

Just like how Mana was great at doing all the chores despite being a *gyaru*.

"You think?"

"Yup."

"Now, talking about you specifically, not all guys—what do you think?"

"It was surprising to hear. In a good way."

"That's good."

The only people I had to buy souvenirs for were Mom and Mana, so shopping was quick.

Torigoe returned after doing her own.

"Um... Here." She handed me a small bag.

"Mana's souvenir, right?"

"No... That's for you."

"Huh? Me?"

"I bought the same one for myself... You don't...have to use it, but I...hope you like it," she mumbled. "I-it looks like this." She showed me hers.

It was a nice key chain.

"Thanks. I'll use it."

"Great."

I had to buy something for her, then. As I was mulling it over, Torigoe noticed.

"Y-y-y-y-you don't have to buy anything for me. I just did it because I wanted to."

"You sure?"

I felt guilty for being the only one to receive something, so I asked what she'd like in return.

"If you really want to, then how about you buy me a drink?"

"Is that really enough for you?"

"It's plenty." She smiled.

It didn't sit right with me, but I bought her a can of juice she liked. She carefully stowed it in her bag.

"Seems we lost the other girls," I said.

"Yeah," she replied.

Keeping my promise with Torigoe, we continued wandering around shopping. We didn't look for the other two, and Himeji is quite reliable, despite everything, so we didn't feel particularly worried.

We wandered around the market, searching together for Torigoe's gift to Mana.

Torigoe wasn't in super-high spirits—or low, either. She was acting like her usual self. We didn't try to force a conversation, and the silence didn't feel awkward.

I glanced in Waka's direction and saw Deguchi was still with her, chatting.

"Do you want to be with older women?" Torigoe asked basically the same question as he did.

"I dunno. Not really."

Sure, there was a special charm that girls my age didn't have, but the reverse was also true. It wasn't as though I'd gotten in deep enough with a girl my age to know I wanted something different, so I wasn't particularly interested in going after anyone older.

"I see. Boys are usually attracted to motherly women. Like moths to a flame."

"I sense bitterness in your tone, Torigoe."

"You think?"

The moth—Deguchi—was merrily chatting with the flame—Waka—as we watched. She must've been at least somewhat pleased to have someone to talk to; that job seemed very dull.

"I just thought you'd also like someone like your sister, Takamori."

I thought we were talking about mother complexes, not sisters.

Although…Mana was as motherly as it could get. She was stern, devoted, and great at cooking.

Wait a second. Do I have a sister complex?

"I mean, I love her, as a sister, but that's way out of my strike zone."

After a while of walking, we found an empty food court and sat down.

"…So what exactly is in your strike zone?"

I shouldn't have said that.

I had never thought about it.

"First of all… Not Mana or any of my relatives. Not anyone too far off my own age… I'd say they'd have to be within two or three years of mine."

"Pretty normal answer."

"What'd you expect?"

Then she started drinking that juice I bought her.

There was still some time left, so we relaxed for a while.

◆Hina Fushimi◆

"There they are!" Ai pointed at Ryou and Shii sitting at a table.

We had lost sight of them after I started arguing with Ai, and it took us a while to find them.

"Let's join them," she said as she walked toward the two.

I grabbed her arm. "Hey, Ai, wanna go buy some gifts for everyone back home?"

"We could do that all together."

I pointed in the direction opposite them. "Look, they're selling something yummy over there!"

"Where do you think you're going?" She brushed my arm off after a couple of steps.

"I told you: We're buying souvenirs."

"…" She stared right at me. "Do you not want to get in the way of those two?"

"That's not…"

That was exactly it. She saw right through me.

"I see… So you want Shizuka and Ryou to end up together."

"That's not it, either… I think."

"What is it, then?"

Ai was completely right. She was always so direct with her words.

Although she didn't admit to liking Ryou, I could tell she was trying to get his attention, to get closer to him again.

"I won't hand him over to her, but still... I don't want to get in the way." I voiced my honest thoughts.

Shii was my friend, and although I didn't know what she might think about it, or how things could turn out, I wanted her to stay my friend. Which was why that sneaky trick I had pulled made me feel so guilty. Ryou wasn't making things clear, so I kissed him to try to fill his mind with me.

Maybe I was feeling anxious after hearing he had dated Shinohara.

So I forced myself on him. It was all me. The mood wasn't even there. And Shii, my friend, was in love with the same person.

"You won't be crying when you lose because you played nice?"

"I'm telling you that won't happen. I just want it to be fair and square."

And I had already cheated that time. I wasn't even sure I deserved to be in the same group for the trip. And then there was that mess the previous night...

I wanted to pretend I hadn't seen what happened today, so I could feel like we were on the same playing field again.

"Fair and square? How childish." She frowned. "That's not possible. What are you even thinking? Of course she'll be mad at you if she loses. And you'll be mad at yourself if you lose. That's how things are." Ai spoke the truth, in a different manner from Shii's. "Are you afraid of Shizuka hating you?"

I knew what she was getting at. I've had people whispering behind my back before. They would even say it explicitly so I could hear it. It was typical. Not only for me; many times I'd heard others bad-mouthing someone else.

That was just the kind of place school was.

And after I understood that, I stopped caring about what other people were saying about me.

But not with Shii.

I had shown my real self to her. I had talked with her about things I'd never told anyone else. She was special to me, like no one else had ever been. No one besides Ryou.

"I'm not as strong as you are, so I might cry… But if Ryou falls in love with someone else, then I want to give him my support."

"Don't fool yourself. You know you want him for yourself."

I do, but…

She really did not mince her words.

I felt we would get in an argument again if we kept going.

"In any case, just let them be for now."

"I have no reason to do that… But okay. I'll do it just this once." Ai brushed her hair in annoyance. I guess she couldn't totally hide her frustration.

I changed the topic back to the souvenirs, and we talked about what to buy and for whom as we walked through the marketplace.

"A key case? That sounds nice," I said once I saw what Ai had brought to the register.

Although, it wasn't cute enough to be considered a gift.

"I'm giving it to Ryou?"

"Bw-wuh?"

"Can't I? It should be no problem, right? I think he'll like it."

I really couldn't take my eyes off her for a second. *I should buy him something, too, then.*

I was amazed that she was so confident he'd like the gift, too. Perhaps she knew Ryou didn't have one already.

"What should I get? Hmmm."

While I was looking at the merchandise on the shelves, someone asked me:

"Excuse me, could you tell me how to get to the station?"

The guy looked very sorry for bothering me. He was about twenty years old.

"Huh? Um, couldn't you look it up on your phone?"

"It's out of battery."

Oh. Makes sense, then. Is he a tourist, too?

"You're here on your school field trip? Wow!" he said as I showed him the way to the station on my phone.

"Hmm, I still don't get it… Would you mind guiding me over there?" He smiled awkwardly.

"Uh… Only halfway there, okay?"

We left the arcade and went out onto the main street.

Then I felt someone forcefully grab my shoulder.

I turned around, scared, but it was Ryou.

"Ryou? What's wrong?"

"Who's that guy?"

Ryou glanced at him.

"He asked me to show him the way to the station, so…"

"I—I already got it, thank you!" the guy said, leaving in a hurry.

Ryou heaved a heavy sigh.

"Are you serious?" He placed both hands on my shoulders and sighed again.

"What's wrong?"

"What's wrong with *you*?" His hands on my shoulders were warm and slightly trembling. "Did no one ever tell you not to follow strangers?"

"I wasn't following him; he was following me."

"Didn't you find it weird in the slightest? Doesn't he have a phone?"

"He said it was out of battery."

"And why would he ask someone who's clearly a student visiting on a school field trip, instead of a local?"

…*Now that you mention it.*

"He was definitely planning to do something to you. He took advantage of your kindness."

Ryou glared in the direction the guy went.

He told me all the other things the man could've done. He could've called a taxi instead. If he didn't have money, he could've asked a taxi driver. He could've taken a bus. The more options he listed, the more embarrassed I felt.

"I'm glad nothing happened. I—I was scared he'd have 'friends' coming after us. Let's go," he said, turning back toward the shopping street.

"Hey, how...?"

"How what?"

"Weren't you with Shii?"

"Oh... I was heading to the restroom and saw you. Where's Himeji been all this time, by the way?" He sighed again.

"Was I really being that careless?"

"You get the award for being the most careless person of the year."

"Wow."

I'm...actually happy about this...

"Sorry for worrying you."

"Don't sweat it. I just wouldn't have wanted to think, *Oh, she'll be fine* and let you go, and then regret it later."

Just wouldn't have wanted to regret it...

"And, like"—Ryou looked away and scratched his head—"I don't like myself that much, you know. Actually, I dislike myself. So I wouldn't want more reasons to."

Ryou insisted he didn't do it for me, but for himself. But I could tell right away he was just trying to rationalize it in some way to play it cool. In any case, the reason didn't matter to me.

"You might be studious, Fushimi, but you can be really careless in the weirdest way."

That got a smile out of me.

"You said it."

"Now, where's Himeji? Don't go your separate ways like that, c'mon."

"Ryou."

"Hmm?"

I grabbed his hand before he could leave.

I could hear my heart pounding faster.

I let out a deep breath, took another one in, and spoke directly, like Ai did.

"R-Ryou, even if you don't like yourself, or even dislike yourself... I like you, just the way you are."

My face was boiling. My knees were about to give out.

All my memories with him flashed before my eyes, like I was about to die.

I hoped he wouldn't awkwardly deflect from what I said. In fact, I'd even prefer it if he outright turned me down if that was the...

"Thank you."

Huh? That's not what I expected.

It was the first time I ever tried directly expressing my feelings, I think.

But...he didn't seem to understand what I truly meant by it. Maybe because the flow of the conversation wasn't going in that direction?

"Let's go."

Yeah... He was acting all normal. He probably thought I only tried to cheer him up because of what he said.

For the love of... I felt like fainting.

"F-Fushimi! Your eyes are twitching; are you okay?!"

I am not!

My heart almost jumped out of my chest! I was literally having pre-death hallucinations! And you...!

"Gosh! You dummy!" I gently beat him.

"What? Why are you hitting me?"

"It's all your fault!"

"You got into this yourself, Careless Person of the Year!"

"Aaargh!"

If this is how you want it, then fine! I'll say it as many times as necessary until you understand! I'll throw all the cliché confession methods at you!

So he wouldn't notice, I carefully grabbed his sleeve.

You dense dummy...

Himeji and Torigoe were waiting for us back at the shopping street.

"It's time to go back to the inn," Fushimi said.

"Hina, where were you? I look away for *one second*, and you..."

Torigoe acted before Himeji could finish:

"Hi-yah!" She dealt a chop right on Fushimi's head.

"Ow! Why?!"

"For following a stranger."

"Ah... Ha-ha... So you saw me." She gave an embarrassed smile.

"Good thing Takamori noticed and ran to help..." Torigoe glanced at me. "I was worried sick."

"Sorry, Shii." Fushimi hugged her tight and stroked her back.

"When I first saw you, I didn't really realize what was happening, but I suspected that guy was up to no good, and got scared, and tried calling the teacher, but by then, Takamori was already running after you..."

Don't explain it all to her.

"Ryou, weren't you going to the toilet?"

"The toilet was on the other side of the main street." *Maybe.*

"Thank you, Ryou."

"Sure," I muttered, averting my gaze.

Himeji grinned and stared at me. "So all that happened while I wasn't looking?" she said.

"Yes, *because* you weren't looking."

"Hey, it's not my fault."

"Just kidding." I chuckled and shrugged.

"I'm sure you were scared out of your mind back there," she said.

How could you tell?

"Good, that's good. That means you swallowed your fear for her, right?"

She made it sound like I was some puny guy standing up without any chance of winning. And she was totally right.

"Hey, we're not asking for our childhood friend to be a fearless knight or some prince, okay? So it's fine as it is," Himeji added. "Now, let's go meet up with Deguchi. Already time to go back to the inn, right?"

"What were you talking about with Waka?" I asked Deguchi on the bus back to the inn.

"Just small talk, y'know? And there I realized I totally have a chance with adult women."

How is he so confident?

But halfway through, a male teacher came and dismissed him.

"He asked Waka if she wanted to go look around the marketplace, and I could tell the guy was trying to flirt with her. So I stuck with them."

Don't get in the way, man.

"I think I'm in love with Waka."

"You're so simple…"

"I had so much fun talking to her, and she seemed to enjoy it, too."

I see. So that's his basis for love.

"Maybe she'll say yes if I ask her out."

"Fat chance."

According to Mana, this sort of relationship wasn't that uncommon in manga, so perhaps the chances of this happening in reality were just low, not nonexistent.

"You think?" Deguchi said, not even disheartened. He took out his guidebook and started flipping through its pages. "Wonder when Waka's turn for bathing is."

"You're not planning anything illegal, are you?"

"I just wanna talk with her after she's out of the bath."

Oh, how pure.

"Takayan, I heard someone asked someone else out today."

"Why do that during the field trip?"

"*Because* it's the field trip. Y'know, perfect chance, good timing. Everyone wants a special event to give them an excuse for it."

Oh, just like Valentine's Day, I guess? Makes sense.

We arrived at the inn and had dinner at six PM. During dinner, the teachers warned us that there was an attempt to get into the girls' rooms the night prior.

"We can't go to the girls' rooms, but they said nothing about the teachers' rooms, eh?"

Deguchi, stop talking like you just found the perfect loophole. They're talking about you there; do you not understand? Learn your lesson.

After dinner, we had free time in our rooms.

They all talked about what they did that day, then asked about mine, and I answered with what basically amounted to a supplementary explanation to what Deguchi had already said.

We turned on the TV as background noise for another round of cards, and after a while, an idol they liked showed up on-screen, and it triggered a conversation:

"...Hey, is that rumor about Himejima true?"

He was clearly asking me. I shook my head. "I don't know. Hadn't heard about it from her."

"It would make a lot of sense."

One of the guys hadn't heard the rumor and asked about it, and another one explained.

"Oh, you mean this?"

He looked it up online, then showed us a message board about the group—specifically one about Aika.

These things really exist, huh?

I never tried looking them up myself.

"They say she went on hiatus due to health issues and then left. She hasn't been doing any idol work since… Most people say she retired."

"You think she…did *that*? You know how they say that's common in the industry."

Everyone else stayed quiet. Probably imagining it.

"That's just an urban legend," I denied, since no one tried answering.

"I guess," someone said.

Talk about Himeji stopped, and they started discussing my other childhood friend instead.

"I saw Fushimi talking with someone from Class A after dinner. You think…?"

"What do you mean?"

"Like he called her out to…y'know…"

Deguchi slapped my shoulder. "Remember what I told you, Takayan? That sort of thing happens all the time during field trips."

"We don't know if that's what they were talking about."

"Sure, I guess."

We were about to move on, when one of the guys next to the window called out to us. "Uh, hey, isn't that them?" He sounded startled, so we all went to take a look.

"Where?" "There, look." "Oh, I see them." "That's the guy from Class A." "And that's Fushimi?" "Looks like them."

It wasn't that unusual seeing Fushimi (apparently) getting asked out.

"Takayan, let's go."

"Huh? Why? We'd get in the way."

"Yes, that's the point."

"Huh? What?"

"What if she says yes?!"

"I don't think it'd have any effect on the outcome if we butt in."

"Stop being so coolheaded for once, man. Our Fushimi's getting taken away! Her smile belongs to everyone! We can't let her get a boyfriend!"

"What's wrong with you?!"

"Takayan, let's gooo!"

What am I, a dog chasing a frisbee?

The rest of the guys also urged me to go, so I left the room.

There was a chance that the guy wasn't actually asking her out, so I thought I'd go near enough just to hear them.

Then I'd confirm that was exactly the case, and then everyone back in the room would get all bummed out it wasn't the dramatic confession they wanted. That's how the cliché goes.

…But if it really was as everyone feared…

The sound of my slippers hitting the floor turned slightly faster.

It was at the parking lot behind the inn. The lot was wide enough to park about thirty cars.

I saw them there, in the distance. Fushimi was in her school tracksuit, with that guy from another class.

No one would come this far away just to chat. Guess I wouldn't be able to go back to the room to tell the guys it wasn't what they thought.

The moonlit parking lot was quiet and empty. I could hear their voices, but I couldn't make out the words.

I tried getting closer by moving from shadow to shadow, behind the cars.

I couldn't jump in to interrupt them—not with the mood of that conversation.

"Remember how we were in the same group last year for the school festival, preparing the café and stuff?"

"Yeah."

I could tell from her voice that she knew what was coming, and she didn't urge him on; she only waited for him to say what he was trying to say.

"Ever since then, I... I've been in...in love with you." You could feel the anxiety in his voice. "P-please, go out with me."

I'd heard of this happening many times before, but only afterward. This was the first time I'd witnessed it in real time.

She answered after a moment of silence.

"Thanks. I appreciate your feelings, but I'm sorry."

I heard a sigh. Like he knew this would happen.

I took a peek at his face to see what kinda guy he was, and it was a classmate from last year, a member of the basketball club, I think, or some other sports club. He seemed charming—handsome, even.

But Fushimi always turned them down. She had always done so, and I had no reason to believe she wouldn't do it again.

Yet I had never heard the reason.

"Could you tell me why?"

"I'm still waiting for someone else to notice me."

"So you already like someone?"

"Yes. That's it."

"It's not a girl, is it?"

"No. I like a boy."

I leaned against a tire and slumped down. Hearing about it after it happens and being present in the moment were totally different, even if the results were the same.

I was both weirdly anxious and relieved.

"…"

If Fushimi started dating someone, then things would change between us. We wouldn't go to and from school together anymore, for starters.

So that relief meant I wouldn't want that to change.

I was glad we had returned to our previous relationship. I mean, if I wasn't, would I really keep commuting with her every day?

Then I remembered what Mana had said a while ago—that I was having so much fun.

I just wasn't really aware of it.

But if Fushimi decided to date someone, I'd put her feelings first, and I'd try to help her out with it… I think.

I heard one of them leave. *Right. Would be awkward to go back together.*

I decided to wait until Fushimi left, too.

"…"

I felt someone watching me. I turned around and found her staring at me.

"Whoa!"

"Ryou…" She sighed. "Didn't your mom teach you not to eavesdrop?"

"No, I…"

How did you know I was here?!

"I could hear you trying to sneak up. Geez." She pouted.

"It's just, my roommates…"

No, that's just an excuse. I didn't *have* to listen to them. I could've just tried to get Deguchi's attention back on playing cards.

"We saw you two out here and wondered what you were doing."

"After everyone I've turned down all this time, you think I'd just be like, 'Yaay! Time to date this rando!'?"

"Well, I don't know about that."

She drew nearer to me, while still crouching, and sat down beside me.

"Your tracksuit's gonna get dirty," I said.

"I'll just wipe it off when I stand up."

If you say so.

"Why did you come all the way here?"

"I was curious as to what you were talking about."

"And what did you think about it?"

"I… Well, that was my first time seeing a live confession, so it got me nervous."

"That's not what I mean." She was hugging her knees. She rested her head on my shoulder. "You saw your childhood friend get asked out by another guy. What did you think?"

"I thought I ought to show you my support if you said yes."

She pinched my side.

"Hey!"

"I don't want your support!" She puffed her cheeks and scooched away. "I grant you the Academy Award for Densest Guy."

What?

I just honestly said what I thought.

Come to think of it, Fushimi was also eavesdropping when Torigoe asked me out.

"I would reaaally HATE it if someone asked *you* out!"

Her frown showed her mixed feelings, perhaps reminded about that fact.

"I would be *so* jealous."

"You would?"

"Totally."

I was one of the few people Fushimi could speak honestly with at school, the only others being Torigoe and Himeji. I could see why being robbed of the right to openly chat with me would make her feel frustrated.

"I think I get it."

"Really? Then you should be getting way more upset at what just happened!"

Then why are your eyes sparkling?

"You can take it slow; I won't run away. I'll wait. Any distance that might open between us will close again; I know it. So keep going at your own pace."

I barely understood what she meant, but it was still reassuring to hear.

I had felt like I had to like someone to earn myself a place in class—or just even in school. To fit in.

"It's bath time for the boys, Ryou. You gotta go."

"Right."

"I'll go back to my room, too."

We stood up, and she stretched.

"Yesterday, you just drank juice, right?" I said.

"..."

For a moment, she looked scared, and she awkwardly turned her head away. I could tell she was sweating bullets.

"I—I said it looked like juice... And juice does look like juice... So I didn't lie."

"I know; I'm just surprised you were so bold."

"F-forget about it!" She hurried toward the entrance.

"I really thought you were drunk. You've become a great actress, Fushimi."

She turned around for just a moment with a smug smirk on her face, then ran away.

©Fly

*   *   *

An intense interrogation was waiting for me back at the room.

They asked what they talked about and what happened there at the end. Everyone was watching out the window the entire time.

It wasn't my place to be talking about it, so I shrugged it all off.

I was surprised at how interested they were in other people's business. I always had this idea that only girls were like that, but it turned out that wasn't the case. Just because *I* wasn't interested in that sort of thing didn't mean that all other guys were the same. Maybe I'm just an oddball. I didn't want to believe it, though.

We waited for Fushimi and the girls to come to our room, but then we got a text saying they decided against it after the teacher's warning during dinner.

All the other guys looked like their souls left their bodies the moment we told them. They were really looking forward to it.

So we decided to go to sleep early, at lights-out.

Once everyone was already in their own futon, I sneakily grabbed my phone to text Shinohara. I didn't want to believe I was weird, so I tried getting a second opinion to support my beliefs. I got a reply in ten seconds.

am I weird?

yes, very

No hesitation.

of course it's normal to be interested in that sort of thing

Still, it didn't sit right with me having a former edgy middle schooler call me weird.

I refrained from telling her she had no right calling other people weird and just stopped texting there.

The following morning was the third day of our field trip.

We had nothing scheduled that day, really; most of it was the bus trip back to school. We arrived at three PM.

We didn't go back to the classroom—everyone went straight home.

Our group stood there until the bus turned around and departed.

Then Deguchi said, "It wouldn't feel right just going straight home."

All three girls nodded in agreement. I also understood the feeling.

"How about we make an album, then?"

"Sounds good," Fushimi agreed with Deguchi's suggestion.

It didn't feel right doing it inside school, either, so we walked aimlessly until we arrived at a nearby park. This was grade-school kid territory, but that'd be later in the day—it was still empty. We sat at the table in the gazebo.

"Ugh, that was heavy…" Fushimi sighed after finally putting down the big bag she brought in addition to her rolling suitcase.

Torigoe and Himeji, too. Why did girls carry so much stuff with them? Deguchi and I only carried a bag each.

We started chatting about things unrelated to the main topic, and then Fushimi seemed to have remembered about it and took out her phone.

"I'll upload the photos to our group chat album. Send any other nice pics you might have."

I wasn't expecting the album-making to be digital-only, actually, but hey, the easier, the better.

"Hee-hee. Look."

"Huh? What?" Torigoe looked at Fushimi's phone, then giggled. "You're making a face."

"No, my face just does that in pictures."

"Oh, I have one like that, too. Gimme a sec... Here."

"Ha-ha!"

They looked like a couple of kittens playing around.

Deguchi gave them a warm glance.

"Takayan, let's show each other's pics, too."

"Don't make it sound weird."

"You get your head out of the gutter, man."

"It's not my fault!"

And so we did the same as the girls.

"What the hell, Takayan?! There's no people in these!"

"Wh-what's wrong with taking landscape pictures?"

"Keep a record of *your* trip, man! Don't feel ashamed about showing yourself!" He poked me with his elbow.

"I am not ashamed of anything."

The only pictures with people I had were the selfie I took with Fushimi, which I hadn't downloaded yet, and the photo with all five of us, which I hadn't saved to my phone, either.

While Deguchi and I chatted, Fushimi and Torigoe stopped talking with each other and instead started staring at us.

I turned to look at them.

"Oh... Please, don't mind us. Go on," Fushimi said.

"It's cute seeing you two boys get along."

"Cute? Aw, shucks... You heard that, Takayan?"

Why do you look so happy about it? Calling guys cute isn't really a compliment... Is it?

"What about your pictures, Himeji?"

"I...didn't take a lot."

She immediately tried hiding her phone, so I grabbed it before she could.

"Hey! Don't just take it!"

"I wanna see what you photographed."

Luckily, she had the photos folder open. There were pics of the dinner at the inn, the snacks in their room, the crackers and buns at the rest stop's souvenir snack shop on our way back...

"Wait, it's all food?"

"A-anything wrong with that?!"

She grabbed her phone back, red in the face.

Come to think of it, she was eating a lot during our trip. She had a hefty serving at the inn and was munching on things the whole time we were at the marketplace. Even when Fushimi or Torigoe held back on eating, she ate as much as, if not more than, us guys.

"I guess you're still growing," I said.

"Hey, that's sexual harassment, Takayan."

"I didn't mean it like that, Deguchi. So the only harasser here is you."

"But just before, you were talking about how Himejima's got the biggest tits!"

"No. That was you."

"Huh, was it?"

The glares of the three girls were cuttingly cold. Silence fell.

Even I was caught in the blast.

"...It's fine. It is true, after all," Himeji said, as if nothing had happened.

Deguchi gulped, making a serious expression.

"See, Takayan? I have a good eye, don't I?"

"Please just let the topic die already."

I didn't want this weirdness to overwrite our nice memories of the trip.

We went back to choosing pictures, and the heavy mood started clearing.

Himeji's pics were mostly food. Mine were mainly buildings and landscapes. The other three had snapshots of people, so it was balanced in the end.

"Huh? No one's uploaded their photos with Takayan but me. Why?"

""" ... """"

Himeji cleared her throat. "I believe it wouldn't be appropriate to upload them to an official shared space."

"Y-yeah. There's only two people in each one, so it's fine if just those two have it," Fushimi added.

Torigoe nodded aggressively.

Despite Deguchi's misstep, the album was safely completed. Just looking at the pictures in there brought to mind the memories of the school trip. I liked browsing it.

Our objective accomplished, we left the park and went home.

We parted ways with Deguchi halfway to the station, then with Torigoe.

The train was still empty, so the remaining three of us got to sit down. Then Himeji took a small paper bag from her luggage.

"Here, Ryou. For you."

"What's this?"

I looked inside it and found a key case.

"It's for me?"

"That's what I said. It's a souvenir."

First Torigoe, now her... Is giving souvenirs trendy among girls now?

"I have one, too." Fushimi smiled. She gave me a plushie of an ugly local mascot no one had ever heard of.

What in the...?

"Thanks, you two."

"Though, I'm sure you don't carry any key other than your house's, so maybe you won't need that."

"That is true, but hey, at least I won't lose it now."

"O-oh..." Himeji looked away, joyfully playing with her hair.

"Ryou, don't forget to use your new plushie, too."

What for?

She was so happy that I couldn't let my skepticism show on my face. I did my best to keep a smile on.

Waka had said the trip didn't end until we were home, so finally, the trip came to a close as I stepped through my front door.

I was taking my dirty clothes out of my bag and throwing them in the washer, when I heard Mana's voice coming from the entrance.

"I'm home!"

"I'm home, too!" I replied as I continued getting things out of my bag.

Mana came to me straightaway. "How was your trip, Bubby?"

"Um, pretty good. I think."

Couldn't really think of what else to say.

"You had a lot of fun, huh?"

"How'd you come to that conclusion?"

"You only say that when you do." Mana seemed very pleased. She peered into my bag and said, "What's this?" as she grabbed the enigmatic plushie I was just gifted, her expression turning dark.

"It's a local mascot."

"Bubby, if this is what you got me, then—"

"No, I didn't buy it. I got it as a gift."

I didn't say who gave it to me, since she clearly was intent on criticizing it.

"You know how some things can be ugly but adorable?"

"Huh?"

"Well, you need a certain charm to it. That's how you excuse the ugliness."

She started nitpicking on it right away. Then she sighed. It sounded like she already knew who gave it to me.

"I still don't get it... What's with her sense of aesthetics? It's too... quirky." She tilted her head.

You know how you sometimes see famous people on TV or the web wearing casual clothing, and none of them look weird? If Fushimi tried that, she'd be lucky to even get a pass as "quirky."

"Just leave it; it's whatever. Not like she gave me something ugly out of spite."

I grabbed the plushie and put it back in my bag. Mana kept on looking through my stuff.

"A key chain and a key case. You bought these?"

You could tell I didn't have any before the trip?

"More gifts."

"They're nice."

Yeah. And useful.

I had to get something for Fushimi and Himeji, too, since I technically bought something for Torigoe.

I took my now weightless bag with me upstairs. Mana followed behind.

"What do you want?" I asked.

"Mmm." She only grinned, then followed me inside my room, too. "Bubby?"

"I know, I know."

You already know, don't you? You looked at everything.

I took out the baby sardines with Chinese pepper and soy-boiled seaweed; it was the local specialty of the place we visited.

"Here, this is for you."

I reached out to hand it over, but before she could receive it, she started clapping and burst out laughing.

"I was right! How mature! Oh, my sides!"

"What's so funny about it? I tried it, and it's pretty good. I thought you'd like it."

"Good, good. You wanted to see me smile, didn't you, Bubby? Good boy."

She started patting my head, and I knocked her hand aside.

"You'd stop making food for me if I didn't bring you something you'd like, wouldn't you?"

"I won't deny that. But really, *chirimen sansho*? For your middle schooler baby sister? Ha-ha-ha-ha... Oh, man..."

I was pretty worried about how she'd react, but this was a good sign. Can never go wrong with food.

"I wanted to see more of your aesthetic sense, y'know?"

Apparently, she didn't appreciate the safe choice.

"Oh, by the way..." She remembered something and started looking through my belongings.

She took out the three love gloves.

"You didn't use them..."

"Of course not."

I obviously didn't leave them there when she gave them to me, but she had foreseen that—she sneaked them in again after I had finished packing my bag.

"Well, you should! What do you mean, 'Of course not'?!" she yelled. She was serious.

"What are you so mad about?"

"When did you become such a naughty boy, Bubby?!" She started hitting me. Pretty hard, at that.

"Hey, stop it!"

"You let the freedom of your trip get to you and stopped being so pathetic and oblivious, and then you...you...!"

"Hold on! You're definitely making some wrong assumptions here!"

Mana didn't even bother to stop and listen. "Who was it? Bubby… Are you really more of an adult than I thought?"

"No, stop asking that."

"Y-you mean…it was a stranger? That's why you didn't use it?"

Mana then finally stepped back, eyeing me like I was some dangerous beast.

"I told you the point of this was to prevent trouble for others! You… you sharpshooter!"

Is that supposed to be an insult?

Then she shoved me away and left the room.

"H-hey! Manaaa!"

No choice. I had to set the record straight.

"Your bubby's still a virgin, just so you know!"

I heard her stop in the hallway.

"So why didn't you use it?"

"Because I never needed it for anything."

"Oh… Phew. Okay, good thing you're still a virgin."

No. I don't think that's a good thing. Not at all.

"Just to be sure, I'm leaving one in your wallet!"

"Stop it already!"

Monday came, and we were asked to write a report about the trip.

I was anxious about it at first, but it turned out we only had to write our impressions of the trip. The guidebook and album would be very useful for this.

Waka asked us, the class reps, to gather everyone's reports by the end of the week.

I took out my guidebook and flipped around. The trip already felt like it was something from the distant past, maybe because it had been so liberating.

"What are you going to write about in your report, Ryou?" Fushimi asked me as soon as lunchtime came.

"I think I'll mostly write about the second day."

"Yeah, that was fun. I'm glad you had fun, too."

"I did?"

"You looked so pleased flipping through your guidebook. Your eyes were like an elephant's. So I guessed you had fun."

An...elephant's?

"What are you doing? Let's go," Himeji said as she stood up, bag in hand.

Go where?

"Shizuka's gone already. She should've waited for us."

"You're coming to the physics room, too, Himeji?" I asked.

"Yeah; should I not?"

"No, I didn't mean to say that."

Torigoe also seems to get along with Himeji, so it should be fine.

I grabbed my stuff as well and stood up, and Fushimi looked at us with sadness in her eyes.

"You're not coming, Hina?" Himeji asked.

"She said she's got plans," I replied.

"Plans, huh. What's up with that?"

"Don't say that."

Himeji was the polar opposite of Fushimi, so she didn't understand why Fushimi kept staying in contact with people she didn't actually want to hang out with. Himeji, for better or worse, listened to her heart. She did what she wanted to and avoided what she didn't want to do. Simple.

We arrived at the physics room. Torigoe was at her usual spot, so I walked to mine.

"If I may ask, why are you sitting so far apart?"

"It's better this way. More relaxing."

"Is it?" Himeji looked back and forth between Torigoe and me.

"Takamori, Hiina should be dropping by later," said Torigoe. "We gotta talk."

"About what? The trip report?"

"No, about the film."

Right. We haven't decided what to do for it yet.

"Come to think of it, Miss Wakatabe did say something about filming a movie and showing it at the school festival," Himeji said.

"Yup. With our current budget, the story should be a modern, mundane story about high schoolers... But that's all we have in mind so far," Torigoe answered.

"Oh, I see." Himeji grinned for a moment.

Oh, man. She's gonna cause trouble. I can feel it.

"Himeji, is there any role you would like to play? I'm doing the script, and Takamori's directing, so."

"Well, should you plebs happen to want me as a star, I would guarantee its success," Himeji said proudly.

Sure thing, Your Majesty.

Though her pride did have some weight to it, given that she was a former idol.

"True, but we already decided Fushimi will play the leading role. You'd have to play a side character; is that okay?"

"What if we make Hina the leading male role, and I'm the heroine?"

The sheer audacity. She was totally shameless in her pursuit of stealing someone else's spotlight.

"Thoughts, Torigoe?" I asked.

"Doesn't sound too bad."

"Not a bad idea if I do say so myself, huh? Considering how flat Hina's chest is, she's perfect for the role."

She was being childish, even. Like a spoiled brat demanding everything be done her way.

I suddenly got chills and carefully turned around, and there I saw Fushimi, peeking at us through the window like in a horror movie.

"But really, Fushimi wants to be the heroine, so please…" I tried making peace before she came in, but her patience ran out before I could finish.

"I will be the leading lady. You do something else," said Fushimi.

"Oh, so I would be the male star?" Himeji retorted.

You could cut the tension with a knife. I knew this would happen. Oh well, nothing could be done now.

I turned to look at Torigoe and saw her holding her laughter.

"They're fighting again…"

I supposed they had done the same in their room during the trip.

"Then let's have a contest, Ai," Fushimi proposed.

"What kind of contest?"

"An acting contest! We'll see who really deserves the part."

©Fly

"Fine with me. I'll crush you."

Things took an unexpected turn.

Himeji already had professional experience in the field, feigning smiles and even voice training for her songs. Probably. Not that I knew.

Fushimi was also in the middle of training. It would be a close competition.

"We'll be the judges. Though, just two of us would be...," Torigoe said.

"Want me to call Deguchi?" I suggested.

"Let's go with that."

So I called him.

While we waited for him, we talked about what they would be acting out and decided they'd re-create a scene from a manga Torigoe had brought with her.

Torigoe explained the scenario:

"You'll be playing the protagonist's friend. You're in the hospital because you were injured right before an important tournament. The protagonist and others come visit you there. Your lines start here with 'Thanks for coming.'"

I see.

"And there's one more thing. She sounds cheerful here, but internally, you're so frustrated you're about to cry," I added.

Both of them nodded.

"Shii, was this friend always cheerful?"

"Yes, that's the kind of girl she is. She's a hard worker, but then she gets injured; that's how the story goes."

Not an uncommon occurrence in sports manga.

"'Sup. What's goin' on?" Deguchi arrived, and we explained the situation. "Oh man, that sounds fun. Who's gonna go first?"

They played rock-paper-scissors to determine the order, and so it was Fushimi first, then Himeji.

"Start after I clap once."

"Got it."

We stepped back, and she sat down on a chair. She gave me a glance, and I began the countdown, "One...two..." Then I clapped.

She was only sitting there, yet I could sense her discouragement. Then she noticed something and turned her gaze.

"Thanks for coming." She received the protagonist and friends with a cheery voice. "Wow, if you were gonna bring me sweets here, I wish you'd brought something fancier."

She acted natural. But then her expression turned grim, as though she was recalling something.

The other characters left. She waved with a smile, and soon after, she put the gift down, her expression showing her true feelings.

She bit her lip and clenched her fist.

The scene ended there, so I clapped once again.

"Done."

"F-Fushimi, you're so good! I felt like I was seeing the manga come to life!" Deguchi said.

"Aw, thank you." She scratched her cheek, then walked over to us. "How was it, Ryou?"

"It's what I expected, I guess."

"Say something good!" She puffed her cheeks.

I tried calming her down while Torigoe asked Himeji to be on standby.

"You're next, Himeji," she said.

"Yes."

Himeji got in position and signaled to me that she was ready.

"Thank you for coming."

Oh, she changed the line up a bit.

I watched with anticipation, but...

"Wow, if you were gonna come here, I wish...you brought sweets instead."

…she just couldn't memorize the lines! Even though they were so short!

It was obvious from looking at her face that she was having trouble remembering them, and her tone was flat, like she was reading from a textbook.

A good actress she was not.

"Himeji. You can stop now."

"Huh? I'm only halfway through… But okay. I suppose that's just how impressive my acting was."

Where's all that confidence coming from?

Was she not aware of it? Now *that* was impressive. Overwhelmingly so.

I turned to look at the other judges, and it appeared they thought the same. We all knew who the clear winner was.

We had agreed that the voting would be announced by standing in front of who we thought the winner was, and so all three of us stood before Fushimi.

"Why?! Are you all blind?!"

It really was impressive how she could get mad after *that*.

"Himeji, don't be such a bad sport. Your acting did impress us…*in a bad way*. Anybody would agree."

"Huh?" She opened her eyes wide. "Th-there's no way…"

"After you said being the star would guarantee its success…," Torigoe said.

"St-stop it!" Himeji got red in the face.

Fushimi smiled broadly and tapped her on the shoulder. "Ai."

"Wh-what?"

"That's just how much better I am. Accept reality."

"Argh!"

Don't provoke her, Fushimi.

They argued anyway in the end, but at least we didn't have to change our plans.

"So...what are we doing, at the end of the day?" Deguchi asked, while Fushimi and Himeji fought a silent scowling war.

"Considering the budget, we're doing a modern-day story with a high schooler protagonist. A short—under thirty minutes," I answered, glancing at Torigoe for confirmation.

She nodded. "That's all we have for now. Any suggestions, Deguchi?"

"Nope," he replied immediately. "I'm fine, as long as it feels like it's a product of our collaborative efforts."

His face looked as though he was really proud of what he had just said.

"Hey, Takamori, did you hear that silly teenager?" said Torigoe.

"Yeah, what a bunch of crap, huh?"

"You said it."

We loners could easily agree on that.

"Heyyy, don't insult me to my face!"

Despite our heckling, Deguchi did have a point.

"A product of our collaborative efforts, huh? I don't think we'll need to make many props if we set the story in school...," I said.

"Set construction usually takes the most time and people," Torigoe replied, "but considering our budget and setting, we could probably make everything with just the five of us."

Having lots of props just for the purpose of having everyone participate in production was putting the cart before the horse.

"Torigoe, have you had any ideas yet?"

"Yeah...some."

She took out her phone to check her notes and listed some themes we could do: romance, sports, friendship, youth. The natural conclusions, considering our limitations.

"Fushimi, thoughts?"

She finally joined us, after having scowled at Himeji for an impressive amount of time.

"We should do a romance story."

Torigoe didn't react well. She had noted it as a possible idea, but she wasn't fond of it, apparently.

"I understand how you feel, Shii. I don't think it's the best idea, either."

"Then why suggest it? Why do you want to do it?"

"Because I think everyone's interested in that topic, and it would be the best to get their attention."

Sure enough. We were right at the center of the demographic for that sort of story.

"So a *love story*, huh?" Deguchi said in English, with perfect pronunciation, which just made it more annoying.

"If we make it completely according to my taste, it'd end up being pretty dark," said Fushimi.

"Same," Torigoe agreed.

"But that's fine, isn't it?" Himeji said, pushing them for it. "We can still do something you'd like."

I guess we could make a bleak romance story.

"Takayan, let's do it. Let's make it depressing as heck," said Takayan.

"Man, why does it always feel like everything's gonna crash and burn when you say stuff like that?"

"Oh, c'mon, trust me just a little."

Fushimi cleared her throat loudly. "Let's have a training camp."

"Training?"

"Er, planning camp. For the project."

"Sounds good."

"Yeah, not bad."

"Can I go, too?" Deguchi asked.

Is there any need for the camp *part? Can't we just plan it all here after classes?*

"Then it's settled!"

"Hold on, I haven't agreed to this," I protested.

"Takayan, this might be your last chance to spend the night with some girls, y'know? Let us have this moment."

This guy always loses the main point.

"I'm sure he's just scared because he's never been to a sleepover."

You don't know that!

But it is true.

I stared at the others, asking with my gaze whether *they* had ever been to one. Fushimi and Torigoe both shut their mouths. No experience from them, either. Which is why they wanted to do it, I guessed.

"Fine. Where are we doing it?"

Mana was busy cooking in the kitchen.

"...Anything I could help with?"

"I can't count on you, Bubby. Just wait in the living room, or you'll get in the way."

Welp. I went to wait in the living room.

It was Saturday, past noon.

We had decided to hold the meeting at my house, so I was anxiously looking out the window from the living room.

"Mama looked so surprised. And happy," Mana said from the kitchen.

I had asked her if some friends could stay over, and she immediately said yes.

"Mana, you make them dinner. I won't be home for most of the weekend for work."

"Got it!"

Then she gave her money for the food, so now Mana was carrying out her assigned duties.

I thought it was weird to be starting so early, but she said preparing food for so many people took time.

"Y'know, I'm having fun with this, too. I never get to cook for a big group." Mana giggled.

You're such a good gyaru.

"So Hina, Ai, Shizu, and the Boss are coming, right?"

"Yes, and one more."

"One more?" she asked, confused.

We had called Shinohara in as well, since she had the same level of knowledge of manga, novels, and films as Torigoe. The more people brainstorming ideas, the better.

It was also a good opportunity for me to give her back the manga I borrowed. I'd already finished it, but Mana got really into it and had already reread it multiple times.

Then the doorbell rang. I put on my slippers and opened the door for my two childhood friends.

"Hey. We're here!" Fushimi waved, smiling.

Beside her was Himeji, who was shaking and trying to press her lips together.

"Ha… Hah… Hey… Hi."

She was giving Fushimi a side-glance and covering her face with both hands, just barely containing her laughter.

"Ai's been like this since we met up today…"

Fushimi… I think she's laughing at your clothes.

She seemed so unaware of it. I couldn't just outright tell her. She'd probably start crying again and saying, "It's not a joke!"

Mana showed up then, too, wiping her hands on her apron. She must've recognized the voices.

"Hina, Ai, nice to ha—" She froze in place.

"H-hey, Mana, are you okay?!"

"Bubby… I just had a bad dream."

Himeji finally let out her cackling.

"Huh? What? What's going on?"

"Mana, it's real life. It's not a dream."

"No… I just can't anymore. Y'know, if a fashionable person was doing this, just to test something out for a week; it'd be okay, but…" I held her up as her eyes rolled back. "E-even if she wasn't going out in that… That's just… No…no way, José."

José...

"C'mere, José," Mana beckoned Fushimi.

Fushimi pointed at herself, confused. "Huh? Jo...?"

Mana, with the sternest expression, took her away. Fushimi blinked repeatedly, innocently unaware of what was happening.

"Is she wearing that unironically?" Himeji asked, finally satisfied by her share of laughter.

"Yes. That's the problem."

"Man... That's the most I've laughed this year." She wiped her tears away and sighed. "It's too funny."

After a while, Torigoe, Shinohara, and Deguchi arrived as well.

My bedroom was too small for everyone, so we held the meeting in the living room.

"Takayan, your house is so...normal."

"Were you hoping for anything else?"

"Takamori, where's Hiina?"

"Oh, she's with Mana."

I glanced at Shinohara and saw she was nervously staring at Himeji.

"..."

Right. She doesn't know about her. Or Deguchi, but he's whatever, I guess.

"Shinohara, this is Ai Himejima... She's my childhood friend, and she just transferred into our high school."

"Nice to meet you," Himeji said with a smile.

I introduced Shinohara as well, and then she whispered something into Torigoe's ear.

"Aika?" Torigoe asked. "No—wait, Mii, get ahold of yourself. I mean, I guess Himeji's first name is Ai, but..."

"I mean that, uh..." Shinohara tugged at her hair, then turned to Himeji. "I'm...Minami Shinohara. I-I-I've been to SakuMome's concerts, and I've even shaken your hand a—a few times... A-a-and we also even t-talked for a bit, but it was a really quick conversation, so maybe y-you forgot... But y-y-you were my favorite. Thank you for everything."

Her eyeglasses were getting a bit crooked.

In reaction, Himeji's smile froze. Seemed like something came to mind.

I was surprised Shinohara knew about her. I thought she was only into manga and novels.

I had no idea how famous Himeji was, but if Shinohara said she was her favorite of the group, she probably had some renown among minor idols. She had a dedicated message board, after all.

What now, Himeji? You won't fool her.

I glanced at her, and our eyes met. She was either asking me to stay quiet or back her up.

"I think you've got the wrong person. I get told that a lot."

"You heard her, Shinohara. Sounds like you've got her confused with some weird minor idol? But you shouldn't bother her."

"Oh, sorry I'm weird." Himeji snorted.

Perhaps my way of putting it was wrong, but she also had the worst timing for her rebuttal. Everyone was listening.

"Himeji, you're..."

...basically admitting to being the idol by saying that.

Now everything was awkward.

"I'm going to the bathroom." With that, Torigoe left.

Deguchi looked like he realized what was going on.

Shinohara also seemed to understand, but she decided to respect her decision and said, "Right, yeah, I mistook you for her" in a monotone.

"Bubby! Get them some tea or something!" Mana immediately scolded me for the empty table as she returned.

"You're right." I stood up and went to the kitchen to pour tea for everyone.

I could hear the conversation going on in the living room.

"Hina… Did you change clothes?"

"Yeah. Mana said she'd burn mine if I didn't, so…"

She did?

I glanced at my sister, and she gently shook her head with a stern look on her face.

"You see, Bubby, it's a sin to let her potential go to waste."

"I get what you mean."

Fushimi's clothes stood out more than she did—they would draw so much attention that people would remember the outfit long after the girl herself.

"Thankfully, she's not leaving the neighborhood, but still." Mana pouted.

We took the tea back to the leaving room, and Torigoe was just coming back from the bathroom, too. We were all reunited at last.

"Takayan, you have a sister?"

"Yeah."

"And she's a *gyaru*!"

"Yeah. She'll be making dinner for us tonight."

"*Gyarus* cook?"

"My sister is great at cooking, actually, as well as at all other domestic chores."

"Wow… A *gyaru* sister that does all the housework… You've got it all."

Setting his last comment aside, I did admire my sister.

"It's been a long time since I've been inside here, and sure enough, nothing has changed," Himeji said while looking around the room.

"Yeah, no renovations for a while."

"I see," she replied as she looked in the direction of my room.

"Well, now that we're all here, it's time to begin our third planning meeting for the school film festival," Fushimi announced.

This is the third? Everyone seemed to think the same, though no one asked the question out loud.

We explained the background to Shinohara first, then started brainstorming ideas.

"Something that's simple to do but still entertaining… It sounds like it will all rest on the screenplay," she said, pushing her glasses upward—the motion certainly conveyed an air of authority on the matter. "Though the first problem is: Not everyone enjoys the same things."

Everyone nodded, paying close attention.

"What do you think makes a good movie?" she asked.

Fushimi answered first. "I always look at the director. You can tell from just that, once you're at my level."

Snob.

"It's mostly about the mood and setting for me, I think. Rather than who's starring or who's making it, at least," Torigoe said. I agreed.

Perhaps it was because I wasn't a huge film buff, but I mostly decided what to watch based on synopses and marketing taglines.

"The starring role, of course. I can even get through a mildly boring movie so long as it stars my favorite actors." Himeji didn't seem to think too deeply about it.

"I'm…not sure."

"Why are you even here, then, Deguchi?"

"Takayan, please, call me Degucchi."

"In any case, seems like we all have different opinions, huh."

"Don't ignore me!"

It was still too early for me to call him by a nickname. I needed time to mentally prepare myself.

Everyone kept on talking about what aspects of movies they liked, and I was in charge of taking notes in the notebook Fushimi had prepared. But we weren't reaching any conclusions to write down.

Fushimi, Torigoe, and Shinohara would not stop talking once the topic changed to their favorite movies and stories, and Himeji's opinions were as simple as ever.

"How's it going?" Mana dropped by. "Here, I brought some of Bubby's snacks."

She brought a basket full of snacks I was saving up.

"Hey, I was—"

"I'll buy you more later, so stop grumbling."

"..." Deguchi was staring intently at her. "A motherly *gyaru*...?" He was almost blushing.

We took a snack break. I went up to my room to clear my mind and look up some manga to use and reference, and while I was doing that, Himeji followed me inside.

"Knock first."

"Too late." She grinned, then sat on my bed. "This room is the same as back then, too?"

"There's nothing that needed to change, so."

"Wonder where you hide the dirty stuff..." She looked under my bed and inside my pillowcases.

"Shouldn't it be Deguchi doing that?"

"So you admit to having it?"

"I guess. Just a tad."

No need to hide it from her. I already knew some of her secrets.

I sat at my desk and skimmed over the manga.

"Shinohara must've scared you back there."

"Yeah... I also remember her."

No cap? I always thought idols never remembered their fans. Perhaps Shinohara was too enthusiastic, or she left an impression some other way.

"She told me something along the lines of 'Seeing what you've accomplished at your age gives me the courage to keep on trying.' Hopefully, she's not disappointed seeing where I am now."

I wondered. I had never been a real fan of someone in that way. Was Shinohara disappointed?

"Even if she is, it doesn't matter. Doesn't change who you are."

I grabbed another manga, still keeping my attention away from her.
This one…isn't really what I'm looking for.

After a while of thinking, she spoke again:

"I ran away from it. I was mentally and physically unstable. I couldn't keep up with my training… I used to want to be an idol so badly, and then…"

"I see."

"That's it?" She sighed, but it also sounded like a sigh of relief.

"I haven't even achieved anything *to* run away from. What you did means something. That you put in the effort and gave it a shot. That much I think is commendable."

My thoughts came out easily, maybe because I wasn't looking at her.

From my point of view, the fact that she was able to put in that much effort was something to be envious of. I didn't even know where to direct mine to begin with.

"I never thought the day would come where you cheered me up."

"Really?"

Himeji stood up. I thought she was leaving, but then she opened my closet.

"I don't have dirty stuff there, just so you know."

"No, that's not it. If nothing's really changed, then maybe…"

Maybe what?

"Oh, there it is! You still have it, Ryou!" Himeji exclaimed as she showed me an all-purpose notebook.

Grade 3, Class 1—Ryou Takamori

That's mine?

"You were keeping it in the same exact place."

"Was I…?"

More like I just forgot about it.

"You don't remember we hid it in here?"

"Hey! We're starting!" I heard Fushimi shout from below.

I wasn't sure I remembered.

Grade 3 was seven or eight years ago.

Maybe I tried to look for it a while after that and forgot where we hid it...although I didn't have any recollection of looking for it. I probably hadn't seen it since then. Pretty normal thing for an easily bored child.

"We'll take a look at it later," she said. So I gave it to her.

Considering we hid it together, I supposed we both wrote something in there, though I had no idea what. All-purpose notebooks in third grade were basically for doodling, so probably nothing important.

We went back to the living room and resumed the meeting.

We listed some works to use as inspiration and suggested the setting for our story based on them, then went back and forth as we pointed out how all our ideas were obviously cribbed. We weren't making any progress.

Once again, I realized how impressive authors were.

"Torigoe's the screenwriter, so can't we leave it to her?" Deguchi whined.

"Deguchi, c'mon. Then what would be the purpose of this meeting?"

"What? Listen up here, Takayan! This is a planning meeting in name only! We're here for a sleepover!"

That's not... I glanced at Torigoe and Fushimi for agreement, but it seemed they sided with the wrong person. They averted their eyes.

It is? You really came here just for a sleepover?

I sighed.

"Okay, then we leave it in Torigoe's hands, and she'll consult us if she has any questions."

Everyone nodded.

"I think I'll have plenty of them, so I'll be counting on you all," she said.

"You can do it, Shii."

"Thanks. I think I'll be consulting a lot with Takamori personally."

Mana's (still there) and Shinohara's eyes lit up.

Fushimi and Himeji stared right at me.

"Well, I am the director, right?" I said. "We could figure out ways to show stuff that's difficult to depict on camera."

Shinohara tilted her head in confusion, so I added, "I mean, with the right camera angles, you could easily make a scene where aliens appear or something."

"Takayan, no way. Aliens? Ha-ha-ha." He laughed, slapping my shoulder.

I brushed his hand off. "It's just an example. Anyway, depending on the shot and the right dialogue, we could make it appear as though aliens are there without showing them on-screen."

It'll look cheap, but it is a cheap film. So.

"Wow! You're a genius, Takayan!"

Not sure your praise makes me very happy…

"So yes, I'll be counting on you, Takamori."

"Shizu, you're so bold," Mana said.

Torigoe cast her eyes down. "I didn't mean it that way…" She grabbed her bangs and stayed quiet.

Mana then left to prepare dinner, and I went with her to help out.

"You're having fun today, Mana."

"Well, it's the first time you've brought someone home other than Hina, Ai, and Shizu, isn't it?"

"Is it?"

"It is! Now I see you're loved by many, Bubby."

"I feel like there are multiple layers of misunderstandings in your statement."

"Not at all. Though I am a bit sad about it, too." She giggled and locked her arm with mine, then gave me instructions on what to do.

I was lining up the plates when Shinohara showed up at the kitchen.

"What's up?" I asked.

"I'm heading out for today," she replied.

"Oh."

"I'm already full, in my chest…"

Oh, is this about Himeji?

"I feel like I'll go crazy if I keep on breathing the same air."

"Don't be ridiculous."

I saw her to the door, and we said good-bye.

"Shino's good, too. Love the cool, glasses type," Deguchi said, staring at the door sadly. He had come with us to see her off.

He really doesn't have a type beyond "girl," huh?

"Why did the Boss leave?" Mana asked once I got back to the kitchen.

"She's a big fan of Aika, and she couldn't keep her mind straight anymore."

"Like, she was almost peeing herself from excitement?"

"Gross, don't say that."

Dinner was ready, and we called everyone to the dining room.

"You're good at cooking, Mana-banana!"

"You can say that again," she said.

"Ryou, you eat like this every day?" Himeji asked.

I nodded. "She made it extra fancy tonight, but her normal cooking is also good."

"You can say that again." Mana puffed her chest.

"Hina's bad at cooking, right?" Himeji said.

"Don't assume. I'm okay at it. Average."

"Oh, no, she's bad," Mana said.

"Yeah, Hiina shouldn't be left alone in the kitchen," Torigoe said.

"That's not true!"

Sorry, Fushimi, but you can't call someone who can only boil pumpkin a good cook.

We put on a variety TV show as background noise as we ate. She had prepared enough for Shinohara, too, but even that portion disappeared in no time.

"That was delicious, Mana-banana."

"You can say that again."

We all did the dishes and then prepared for a bath.

"Hina, let's go in together," Himeji said.

"Whaaa—?"

"Let's go, Hina! All three childhood friends, together again," Mana added.

"N-no!" Fushimi glanced at both their chests, then strongly shook her head.

"Why? No need to feel ashamed about your flat chest."

"Argh! Try saying that again with one yourself!"

"C'mon, it's fine! You're slender, that's all!" Mana giggled, poking her. She totally knew what she was doing.

"This is breast harassment!" Fushimi showed her teeth in an attempt to intimidate them.

Then Deguchi placed his hand on her shoulder.

"Fushimi, I'm totally fine with it."

"Stop it!"

The disgust on her face was very real. Deguchi was deeply affected by that—she never showed her true face in the classroom.

"I never knew she could make that expression."

"She must've been really freaked out."

"I think I could survive just by seeing a pretty, good-mannered girl glaring at me in disgust like that…"

His tastes in women knew no boundaries.

And anyway… Was no one thinking about taking a bath one at a time?

"Hiina, let's go in together."

"Yeah, I'm fine with you, Shii."

Shinohara had said Torigoe concealed her actual size. I wondered if that was true. Considering Fushimi had accepted right away, perhaps not.

"Takayan, let's go in together."

"Why? Go in by yourself. We both won't fit."

"I figured."

Mana and Himeji went in first, then Fushimi and Torigoe, then me, and Deguchi last.

"Takayan, let me go in first."

"Why?"

"I wanna take that bath while the pretty-girl element of the water is at its purest."

"You two are gonna be taking a shower. We'll drain the bath," Mana said, her eyes narrowed. "I would've kicked you to death already if you weren't Bubby's friend."

"Calm down, Mana."

"Tell him that!" She puffed her cheeks.

"No, I mean, you'd only be giving him what he wants."

"Wha—?! Blegh!"

Deguchi didn't seem to care. He had a mind of steel, apparently.

"Takayan… I hope you don't mind if I cry all over your pillow."

…Or not.

Either way, it's your fault. Hopefully, you'll learn from this.

"The girls all sure get along, huh?" Deguchi said once Himeji and Mana left for the bathroom.

I could kinda tell that relationships between guys were a bit different, but to be honest, I wasn't really sure, so I just kept my mouth shut.

"Is Mana-banana pretty without makeup, too?" Deguchi asked.

"I see her without it most of the time, so I'd say I prefer that."

"Huh."

I wondered what Himeji looked like. She hadn't changed a lot since then, but I had only ever seen her with makeup since our reunion, so maybe she'd look different.

I could hear Mana giggle in excitement and Himeji trying to calm her down.

Fushimi, Torigoe, Deguchi, and I watched TV absentmindedly, when suddenly, Torigoe took out her phone and started typing.

She grumbled with a frown and whispered, "Hmm... Not bad?"

I was sure the screenwriter would have it the hardest out of all.

"Hey, Torigoe, anything I could help out with?"

"No."

Okay...

"I have an idea of what the dialogue should sound like, but I don't know anything about how to structure a story," Fushimi said, sad that she couldn't contribute more.

We had no choice but to wait for her to come up with the scenario.

Mana and Himeji came out of the bathroom, and Fushimi and Torigoe went in.

"What is it?"

I was staring at Himeji. Her usually pretty face with makeup was now plain, like a smooth boiled egg.

She definitely looked more like she did back then without makeup.

"Just thinking about old times."

"Okay?"

Deguchi and Mana were talking about the TV show. They both were followers of the drama and seemed to be having fun.

Then I wondered where that notebook I gave Himeji ended up.

It might be a sort of time capsule, so I really wanted to go through it.

I brought it up to her, and she went to the living room. I followed.

Mana and Deguchi didn't seem interested, or perhaps they were more interested in the TV drama, so they stayed in the living room.

"Ryou, do you remember what we wrote here?"

"Not at all."

The handwriting for my name on the cover was terrible. I didn't have pretty handwriting then, either, but it was much better now compared to back in grade school.

Himeji opened it up and flipped through its pages. Most of it had doodles: of monsters, robots, or anime characters I liked back then.

"Hee-hee, you were adorable."

"This is a pretty normal notebook for a third-grader, okay?"

"Oh, what's this, an umbrella?" Himeji said with excitement in her voice. "Look!" She drew nearer to me and pointed at the drawing.

Her hair was still wet, and I could smell Mana's conditioner; it felt weird to catch the scent coming from her.

I glanced down at where she was pointing and saw an umbrella drawing, with both our names on either side of the handle in sloppy handwriting.

"We were just kids. But so what? Right…? Ryou, you…liked me, didn't you? But that doesn't matter now. Right?" She fanned herself with her other hand.

"I…liked you?"

"You can very clearly tell from this."

The handwriting was the same as those on the pages before it, so most likely, I wrote that.

"Maybe I did, back in third grade."

"Oh, so now you're playing cool?" She smiled.

"I'm not playing at anything…"

"But I remember." Her eyelids lowered, nostalgic; her fingers traced the shape of the umbrella. "I knew you liked me. And I think you knew I felt the same way."

Really? Wait. Hmm?

"Himeji, did you like me?"

"…" She stared at me with a serious face for a few seconds. "I don't understand what you're asking."

"Pretty much exactly what I said."

"I don't feel trapped by the past, you know," she said. "Don't bring up stuff from third grade."

"But you started it."

What are we doing here, then?

"We loved each other," she whispered, staring straight into my eyes. "...Or so you thought."

She was hell-bent on not accepting it.

"It's all in the past. It doesn't matter now who liked who back then... in my opinion," I said.

I felt the same way regarding Fushimi. She was intent on keeping any and all promises we made back then. That's just how she was, but she didn't need to feel chained by those things we said in the past.

"I can't believe *you're* the one saying this."

"I'm just saying we shouldn't worry about anything written here. We shouldn't be trapped, like you said. And thinking back on it now, any 'love' we might've felt as grade-schoolers is nothing big."

"Fine. It's fine." She stopped me. "I'm just glad to know that I wasn't the only one who thought so back then."

She accepted it in the end. Then what was all that just now for?

"We're living in the present. Let's leave the past in the past." I'd really wanted to say that out loud.

"True. But you know, you'll still like the same person if that love doesn't end."

"I guess?"

There were many ways for love to end—you might start disliking the person, they might reject you, you might give up...

Of course, I didn't think this former idol could possibly still be chained by the past.

Then Himeji placed her hand on my thigh and drew her face nearer. "Do you think my first love is already over?"

"I dunno" was the only thing I could say as I looked away.

I didn't even know if *I* was her first love in the first place. How could I know the answer to that?

"Ai… What are you doing?"

The voice came from near the front door. Fushimi, who had just finished showering, was standing there.

She was smiling, but there was something dark about it.

"What? We're just talking."

"Aren't you too close? Don't you find that weird? It is a bit weird, don't you think?"

"Is it, though?" Himeji played dumb.

Fushimi's veins on her forehead were popping. "J-j-ju-just get away from him alreadyyy!" She shouted so loudly that probably everyone in the neighborhood heard.

Her voice training sure was working.

I, for one, understood how serious the situation was, so I pushed Himeji away.

Fushimi was pouting and furious. I could see her eyes starting to well up; her lips were trembling. Then she turned around and ran into the hallway.

"Fushimi!" I moved without thinking. I stood up from the sofa and tried following after her, but someone grabbed my arm.

"Where are you going?"

"Where do you think?"

Didn't you see her?

I had more I wanted to say to her, but the words were stuck in my throat.

"You can't do anything about her now."

"Maybe, but still."

How long had she been standing there? Was Himeji aware of it the whole time?

"You ought to learn already that kindness can sometimes only make wounds deeper."

"What in the world are you—?"

"That's how you are, Ryou. I get it. That's your personality, and it's definitely virtuous. But you know, you're oblivious about your actions, unlike Hina, and you only do it within a closed circle of friends." Then she finally let my arm go. "Do you like Hina?"

"What's with the sudden question?"

"If you like her…if you *love* her, then go." She snorted.

I sighed, then walked away from the living room.

"Wha—?! W-wait! You're really going?!" Himeji exclaimed.

"Shut up! I've had enough of that like and love crap! Why would that be the entire basis for my decisions?! Plus, you have no right to order me around!"

"Bwuhh… Th-that's not what I was expecting!" She kept on shouting as I left. "That's exactly why everyone is so upset, jerk!"

I understood Himeji was saying those things for my own good, in her own way, but I thought it was better to clear up any misunderstanding Fushimi might've had sooner rather than later.

I saw her shoes still in the entrance. I looked up.

I walked up the stairs and opened the door to my room carefully. There was something under my blankets.

I knew you'd be here.

I let out a sigh of relief.

Fushimi poked her head out to check who had come in, then immediately hid again.

"Hey."

She scooched over like a worm, blanket and all, allowing me some space on the edge of my bed.

I guess I'll sit, then.

For a moment, I worried about her getting weird smells from my bed. She huffed, then spoke quickly. "Why did you come?"

"It's my room. What's so wrong about me coming into my room?"

I sat down on the bed, and the worm turned her back to me.

"You were flirting with Ai."

"That was all Himeji's doing."

"You were about to kiss."

"I wouldn't."

"Liar." She spoke clearly. "It was you who was in the gym storage room doing naughty things with the transfer student, wasn't it? It was you who was with her."

...So she knew.

"We didn't do anything."

I didn't know what to say, but apologizing didn't feel like the right answer. I had to think for a while.

"Really?"

"Really. Whoever spread the rumors made it all up."

"I trust you."

"Thank you."

I patted my blanket. Then she showed her face.

"..."

She was still sulking. "Keep going."

She wants me to do the same but without the blanket?

I patted her head, and her grumpiness quickly disappeared.

"I was hoping to just have a fun pajama party tonight."

"Sorry."

"I accept your apology, but it's not your fault. Kinda."

Which is it?

"If only there was a villain in this story, then we'd just have to defeat them. What a dilemma...," she whispered, and soon enough, she fell asleep.

It was ten PM. Not exactly time to sleep when you've planned to hold a pajama party, but I supposed she usually went to sleep at this time.

I heard people talking downstairs. I grabbed a game console from my closet and went back to the living room.

We played a four-player game. Deguchi was familiar with it, so he explained how to play it to Himeji and Torigoe.

"Bubby, where's Hina?"

"She fell asleep."

"Whaaat? That's not how you spend a sleepover!" She lifted a brow. "What did she even come here for, then? Geez. Oh, where is she sleeping? My bed?"

"No, she just took mine."

"Hmm? And what were you two doing just before?"

You don't need to look at me like that.

"Nothing."

"Yeah, I guessed. It's you we're talking about." She grinned.

I took a bath while they were gaming. Well, not a bath. A shower. They really did as Mana warned.

I wondered what else could be in that notebook I hid with Himeji. I (supposedly) made a bunch of promises with Fushimi, so maybe I did something similar with her, too.

Once I got out of the bath, while everyone was enthusiastically gaming, I grabbed the notebook and looked through it in the living room.

"Mana-banana, that's cheating!"

"It's not; this is just my style."

"Ah! Shizuka, don't!"

"Sorry, Himeji. All's fair in love and war."

It was a retro game console, but it was still a blast playing multiplayer. Mana, Fushimi, Himeji, and I used to play it all the time back then.

I looked through the notebook as I listened to their bickering.

Most of the notebook's content was badly drawn doodles or badly written scribbles. Pretty normal for a third-grader, I think.

But halfway through, the handwriting became more similar to my current one. There was no date to be found, but I supposed I had grabbed it again later on for note-taking, seeing as it had some pages left.

And just as I thought, there were promises written there. That we'd go to the same college or that we'd hold hands. All of the same ones Fushimi had been talking about lately.

"Oh, I really took notes on my promises to Fushimi."

Good. Now I would be able to know whether the things she brought up were real.

I went back and joined everyone in the game. All the noise also woke up Fushimi, and she joined us, too. We played until late at night.

"Aren't we bothering the neighbors?" Deguchi asked.

"It's fine," both Fushimi and Himeji said.

"We've got Mana here."

"I've heard Mana's famous throughout the neighborhood," Himeji said.

"Hee-hee. You flatter me."

Everyone in the neighborhood knew and loved my sister, and they forgave her for everything.

Torigoe was already dozing off, so she and the rest of the girls left the living room.

"Takayan, let's go to sleep, too."

"Yeah. Good night."

"Hold on. Where's my bed?" he asked.

I glanced at the sofa.

"There? I'm sleeping on the couch?"

"If you don't like it, then go home."

"You monster!"

"I'm serious. We only have three extra futons."

"Let me sleep on your bed. And you go sleep with your sister. There, all solved."

Uh, nothing solved.

"Okay, how about I arrange some cushions into a bed for you?"

"That's the kind of good hosting I was looking for."

Yeah, I couldn't have a guest sleep on the floor, so I grabbed some cushions and took them upstairs to my room.

"Your room is so empty. Very Takayan-y."

"You think?"

I lined up the cushions beside my bed, and then he went to lie down on them.

I got on my bed and turned off the lights.

It smelled good. Probably because Fushimi was just sleeping there. It had been only one hour, and still that was enough to make it feel like it wasn't my own bed.

"Takayan, you sleep with the lights off?"

"Yeah."

"I prefer a nightlight."

"As they say, when in Rome, do as the Romans do."

"Damn Romans."

I chuckled.

"I hope the film turns out well. Y'know, I've never tried too hard at events like this. It's like…I'd feel a bit embarrassed about taking it too seriously." I knew exactly what Deguchi meant. "I mean, like, I won't say it's *cooler* to not take things seriously, but it feels like I'm just doing what someone else tells me to do, and I don't like that. Like I'm not being asked to do it; I'm being forced to do it."

My eyes finally got used to the darkness, and I started making out the silhouettes of the ceiling and furniture.

"It was Fushimi who came up with the idea of making a film. So it's true, in a way, we'd just be doing what she tells us to do."

"But it doesn't feel like it. You two class reps listened to everyone's opinions. And it also matters who suggested it. I think more people would've shot it down if someone else had said it. It's like how you react differently to a joke when a popular comedian says it than when some guy in your class does."

That's a thing?

"What I mean is: It's important that you two are at the center of this, Takayan. It makes me feel like I can take things seriously. If only this once."

Was it because I was the king of no motivation? The fact that even I was looking forward to this lured the guys who thought similarly into following me...

"Okay, this is getting embarrassing. Go to sleep," I said.

It took no time for me to hear Deguchi sleeping.

Having someone tell me all this made me feel like being class rep wasn't so bad after all.

I also hoped things would go smoothly with the film.

In that odd time frame where you can't consider it morning or noon, I woke up and ate a breakfast made by Mana.

Everyone was already up and ready to go.

"Thank you for having me," Torigoe said with a bow before leaving.

"I'll see Torigoe off to the station. Bye," Deguchi said with an audacious expression, then hurried behind her.

"See you tomorrow, Ryou."

"See you."

Fushimi and Himeji also left.

"Now we're all alone, Bubby," Mana said, sounding lonely.

I felt the same.

In the end, we made no progress at all on the project. But it was fun, and that's what mattered.

Mana and I tidied up the living room and kitchen, then I went to clean up my room. Not much happened there, so it went fast.

Do you still have the notebook? Himeji texted me.

yes

Ok. Good.

Then a question popped up in my mind.

do you remember why we hid it together?

Why? Because it's full of stuff between you and me.

"Between you and me…?" I read out loud.

Then I flipped through its pages again.

…*These are all with Himeji?*

was there anything we wrote together besides the umbrella thing?

Look near the end. We filled it up with childish promises.

Going back home together. Holding hands. That stuff…was with Himeji? What?

you mean these aren't promises i made with fushimi?

She had been replying quickly before that, but then she left that on read. Why? Huh?

Then I got a call. From her.

"Hello?"

"What do you mean, promises you made with Hina?"

"What do I mean? I…"

I explained to her that Fushimi had been bringing up old promises lately, and they lined up perfectly with what was written in the notebook.

"If you made those promises after I transferred, then fine. But as far as I remember, we were the only ones who made those promises before that."

I only made promises with Himeji…?

There was no way I had made any promises with Fushimi after middle school. We didn't even start talking with each other until just recently.

So then after Himeji transferred away? That wasn't too long ago.

"Maybe I made some with her, and you just don't know, right?"

It was just that I forgot about them… Right?

"She would've told me all about it if that was the case. It's also weird how it's all the same ones we made."

Could it be…that I actually hadn't forgotten about any promises with Fushimi?

"Hina has always been good at imitating me."

We were always together back then, and we did everything together, too.

"If it's true that you don't remember, then we've got a few contradictions on our hands."

Himeji reached the same conclusion as me.

"The promises in that notebook are between us."

Which meant…

"Maybe you don't remember any promises with Hina because you didn't make them in the first place."

She said it straightforwardly.

"And clearly, it seems you did not make any."

I took my sixth-grade math notebook out from my desk, as basis for a counterargument.

If who I liked back then wasn't Fushimi, but Himeji…

And the promises Fushimi said I made with her I had already made with Himeji…

I found the notebook. One of its pages was ripped out.

When we get into high school, I'll have my first kiss with Hina.

The words still made me shudder in embarrassment.

Does that mean that I stopped liking Himeji and switched over to liking Fushimi? That's…pretty heartless and shallow of me.

"Hey, Himeji, I really think I made those promises with Fushimi in sixth grade."

She sighed.

"Okay. That's it, then. And to think we were exchanging letters still back then. You playboy."

She spoke in a mocking tone.

"I apologize for that. But… Huh?"

My finger was on the "when we get into high school" part.

"But what?"

Something was off. I flipped a few pages before and after, then went back to it.

This isn't right.

When we get into high school, I'll have my first kiss with Hina.

This isn't my handwriting.

Afterword

Hello there, I'm Kennoji.

We quickly reached Volume 3, and it is all thanks to your support. Thank you so much.

We even had to reprint Volume 2, due to its popularity, so here I am, anxious to hear how the reception for the third one turns out.

So in this volume, we have the new heroine who appeared at the end of the last one, joining Fushimi and Torigoe's circle and going on the school field trip with everyone.

We also have the appearance of Deguchi, one of my favorite characters, who became friends (?) with them. There was a similar character in my other series, *I Time Traveled to My Second Year of High School*, and they are very useful. They allow for a different male perspective from the protagonist and round out the story in general. They also end up as comic relief most of the time, so I really like and appreciate how their roles can be used in so many ways.

A lot of series usually enter summer vacation by the third volume, but here we're still around June. Which means summer vacation is coming next, but as you can see, our characters are living out their youth at a slow-but-steady pace, and they will keep continuing like that.

Many, many people helped in the production of this volume, and I thank you all. I am sorry for not thanking everyone individually, but I really appreciate all your hard work.

I hope you look forward to what's coming next in the story.

KENNOJI